"I know everything about you."

A curious smile curved her lips. "Ain't so?"

"I know you like pineapple sherbet, reading to children and you can't help caring about everyone more than yourself."

"And I know you like my *grossmammi*'s chocolate chip cake. More than that, I know what's most dear to your heart. You're a fixer, Zachary Graber. You fix everything and everyone around you. It's your greatest desire for everyone to be their happiest."

He couldn't tear his gaze from her. Did she have any idea how important she was to him?

"What you've done for your father… This place—the horses—has been his life. Thanks to you, it'll be ready when he's well."

Guilt stabbed, long and hard. He had to look away from the trust and admiration in her eyes. He needed to come clean and tell her.

Tell her he wasn't the man she thought him to be.

But if he did, she might walk away.

And that wasn't a risk he was willing to take.

Cathy Liggett is an Ohio girl who never dreamed her writing journey would take her across the world and to Amish country, too. But she's learned God's plans for our lives are greater and more creative than the ones we often imagine for ourselves. That includes meeting her husband at a high school reunion and marrying three months later—nearly forty years ago. Together, they enjoy visiting kids and grandkids and spoiling their pup, Chaz.

Books by Cathy Liggett

Love Inspired

Her Secret Amish Match
Trusting Her Amish Heart

Visit the Author Profile page at LoveInspired.com.

Trusting Her Amish Heart

Cathy Liggett

LOVE INSPIRED
INSPIRATIONAL ROMANCE

LOVE INSPIRED®

INSPIRATIONAL ROMANCE

Recycling programs
for this product may
not exist in your area.

ISBN-13: 978-1-335-58597-4

Trusting Her Amish Heart

Copyright © 2022 by Cathy Liggett

Love Inspired
22 Adelaide St. West, 41st Floor
Toronto, Ontario M5H 4E3, Canada
www.LoveInspired.com

Printed in U.S.A.

When thou passest through the waters,
I will be with thee; and through the rivers,
they shall not overflow thee:
when thou walkest through the fire,
thou shalt not be burned;
neither shall the flame kindle upon thee.
—*Isaiah* 43:2

To my writing buddies and forever friends—
Shelley Shepard Gray, Hilda Knepp,
Julie Stone and Heather Blake Webber.
My story wouldn't be complete
without you.

Chapter One

"Did you bring me something for the pain?"

As Leah Zook carried a small tray into Ivan Graber's bedroom, her heart wrenched at the sound of his groaning voice. After placing the tray on his nightstand, she settled into the ladder-back chair by the older man's bedside. She couldn't help but notice how the glow from the lamp cast even more shadows on the widower's already ashen face.

"I'm sorry, Mr. Graber, but it's not yet time for another pain reliever."

She winced, wishing she had a more comforting answer for him. Especially since it was close to bedtime, and it wasn't the first time that he'd asked the same question that evening.

"But before I go home, I do have a few graham crackers here for you. And I brought you some water and iced tea, your choice."

She was happy to accommodate him in any way she possibly could. The owner of Sugarcreek's Graber Horse Farm had been through quite a lot in the past weeks since his accident with an uncontrollable, untamed horse.

"No graham crackers." The gray-haired man shook his head. "Just a drink of water."

"All right then," she conceded softly.

His hands trembled weakly as he reached out for the glass, and her heart broke for him all over again. She could tell his fractured ribs were giving him a great deal of discomfort as he feebly lifted his head up from the pillow and took slow sips of water. All the while she couldn't help thinking how much the accident had changed him from the man that she'd started working for six months earlier as his cook and housekeeper.

During her first weeks on the job, she'd found Ivan Graber to be as cantankerous as they came—as feisty and unwilling to yield most times as his unbroken horses. But over time she got used to his ways, even comfortable enough to fondly tease him about his gruffness.

Now here he was, handing her the glass and settling back down under the light sheet with a labored, defeated-sounding sigh that was so unlike him.

"I still can't believe how that horse took me for a ride. Almost thirty years of training horses and I've never gotten hurt so bad. I don't know what I did wrong."

Ever since the accident, he'd been questioning himself. Since then, too, she'd been trying to hearten him.

"Sometimes horses, well, you know, they can get mighty spooked."

"*Jah*, it was bucking and bolting, and I couldn't get it under control. I only wish I would've gotten thrown off from the start." He grimaced. "It would've been better than being yanked around the pen with my foot stuck in the stirrup."

She felt sick to her stomach every time she remembered how she'd come outside to hang laundry and saw him being dragged. Then watched as he got tossed to the ground when his foot finally did break free. Dropping the basket of wet clothes, she went running to his aid. But before she even got to the pen, the wild horse stomped on his fallen body. Along with a badly sprained wrist and multiple fractured ribs, he'd suffered an ankle injury that was diagnosed as a sprain as well—until a week later when the ankle continued to get worse and more tests were run. Then emergency surgery was scheduled right away. His ankle had been bound in a non-weight-bearing cast ever since.

"I'm just thankful I happened to come outside when I did."

"And now you're not only doing my laundry and cooking, you're my caregiver too. Not exactly what you agreed to."

"I don't mind, Mr. Graber. Not at all."

"It seems caregiving is something you've got a real knack for. Your *grossmammi* sure praised you when you moved in next door to take care of her until she passed. You did *gut* by her."

When she was younger, Leah had only imagined herself taking care of a husband and a houseful of *kinner* one day. Yet so far, that hadn't been the path that *Gott* had laid out for her. The older she got, now almost twenty-three, the more unlikely it seemed that it ever would be. Not that she liked to think that way, but sometimes it was best to accept the plain facts.

"Honestly, *Grossmammi* did *gut* by me," she confessed. "And I don't know if you know this, Mr. Graber, but before I moved here from West Union, I was the one in my family who took care of my parents during their final years as well."

She thought her comment would be reassuring. However, Mr. Graber's eyes suddenly grew wide. It took her a moment to realize why.

"Oh, but, Mr. Graber, my grandmother and parents were older than you and not in as good health. But you? You're going to be just fine," she said assuredly. "It'll take some time, but before you know it, you'll be up and about and caring for your horses and training once again."

She prayed that her words were true, especially thinking how they both had dreams that tugged at their hearts. For Mr. Graber, it had always been training horses. And for her— remembering the few times before the accident when she'd had a chance to tutor reading to children, her heart lightened momentarily.

"We're going to get back to our same routines, Mr. Graber. I promise you," she vowed confidently.

"You sound like you mean what you're saying." Mr. Graber's expression brightened some.

"I do. And I don't make promises lightly." Surely not like her older brothers and sister and the former love of her life had. But why was she even thinking about them when they were four hundred miles away? Focusing on the man in front of her, she reached out and checked Mr. Graber's forehead mostly out of habit. She was happy that it was cool to her touch.

"You know, Leah, you're *verra* much like the *dochder* that Marion always hoped for."

Mr. Graber very rarely mentioned his deceased wife's name. Even more uncommonly did he ever say anything the least bit sentimental. Surprised and touched by his comment, she felt a swell of emotion in her throat. In an odd way, she'd been feeling strongly attached and protective as if Mr. Graber was family too. It wasn't until now, hearing him say the word daughter, that she realized why. As a young girl, she'd been powerless to help her *daed* when tragedy struck their family. Though Mr. Graber's situation wasn't the same, she sensed he was on the verge of losing his joy just as her father had. Maybe *Gott* wanted her to make a difference for him in a way she couldn't for her *daed*?

"I *verra* much appreciate you saying that, Mr. Graber."

She had to smile when he shrugged in response as if he hadn't said anything at all.

"So…" She swiped at a teardrop in the corner of her eye. "I'd be happy to read to you if you'd like. I have a book about horses." She patted the copy of *Black Beauty* in her apron pocket.

"Another time. I'm getting sleepy."

"For sure."

Though she always considered reading to be a comfort, a wave of relief flitted through her.

She was so exhausted, and her vision was beginning to cloud. Again. Mr. Graber's face... the tray she'd held in her hand...the light from the lamp... Suddenly everything was blurry. Which had to be from tiredness, didn't it? From worry and fatigue? The problem had started around the time of Mr. Graber's accident. Or was it before? With everything going on, she'd lost track and there hadn't been a minute to think about herself.

"I'll leave the tray here in case you get thirsty in the middle of the night," she said.

She started to get up, but Mr. Graber stopped her. "Before you go, is Matthew taking care of the horses? Training the one I just purchased?"

"He's, uh..." Leah cleared her throat. "He's trying."

Her answer was a definite stretch of the truth. Knowing Mr. Graber's oldest son as she did, she was sure Matthew *would* try to help if he could manage to find a free moment in his busy life. Every time Matthew promised to stop by, he flaked, which she completely understood. That's why she'd added feeding the horses and mucking the stalls to her own list of duties. But, Matthew's *daed* wasn't as understanding.

"Matthew needs to do more than try," Mr.

Graber fumed. "I'm not making any money right now to pay for extra help, you know."

Leah did know and that's why she'd paid herself as little as she could live on in the past weeks. She knew, too, that Mr. Graber wasn't one to accept free assistance from any Amish neighbors.

But, like her cousin Catherine harped at her, Leah was also aware she couldn't keep up her pace. Maintaining everything inside and outside Ivan's house, along with nursing him, was far too much to handle. Her aching bones were proof of that. Even so, she still cringed thinking how she'd made a risky decision by reaching out to Zach Graber in Indiana. But was there any other choice? Mr. Graber's distant son seemed her only hope.

"There may be a chance your other son could help."

"Zachary?" His expression grew even more grim. Leah realized too late that for reasons unknown, it was the first time she'd ever heard his other son's name cross Ivan's lips. "He doesn't like horses, and I've done fine without him the past five years. I can do the same now."

Leah couldn't have been more thankful for the summer evening breeze that ruffled the half-open blinds at that moment. The wisp of air brought a tinge of coolness to the spike of warmth in her cheeks. Given Mr. Graber's reply, she hoped he never learned that she had attempted to contact Zach. Not that it was likely she needed to concern herself with that anyway. As it was, she still hadn't heard back from him. And hadn't Matthew been vague about whether his brother would come? If she was smart, she'd give up on Ivan's long-lost son and move on somehow...some way.

Even so, she thought she should apologize to Mr. Graber for upsetting him. Yet by the time she stood and closed the blinds completely, he had drifted off to sleep. Instead, she said a silent prayer over his bed, yawned an amen and turned out the lamp before heading into the kitchen.

Subtle pastel colors of dusk had lit the kitchen before she'd gone in to take care of Mr. Graber. Now, only the glimmer of the full moon seeped in the kitchen window. Still, there was enough light for her blurry eyes to spy some dirty dishes in the sink. But those would have to wait until morning. Her body was too heavy with fatigue, so tired she could barely see.

Removing her apron, she started to gather up her quilted bag when a disturbing sound from outside stilled her movements. Paralyzed, she stood blinking at the kitchen door, desperately trying to focus her eyes.

Suddenly, the noise came again. Footsteps!

All at once her heart quickened, nearly beating out of her chest. The year before, a prowler had come stalking Ivan's place, attempting to steal a horse. Had someone thought his house was an easy target now that he couldn't defend himself?

Forcing her legs to move, she tiptoed toward the stove. She blindly groped into the air, until her hand landed on a cast-iron skillet hanging on the kitchen wall. Stealthily removing the skillet from its hook, she recalled what she'd read about scaring off coyotes. Be loud. Be noisy. Have something to strike with, if necessary. Surely that had to work for human predators too?

Her every limb trembled as she inched to the middle of the kitchen. Eyes cast toward the door, she couldn't see the doorknob turn but heard the sound. Her hands were shaking as she lifted the skillet over her head, ready to strike. The door was pushed open, and as a shadowy image appeared, she opened her mouth, attempting to scream. But only a frightened whimper came out.

With all her might she swung the skillet, aiming for the blur in front of her. But she hit nothing, which threw her completely off balance. She went flying. Flailing. Falling forward.

* * *

Zachary Graber hadn't played basketball for years. So he was very thankful that he could still sidestep quickly enough to dodge a large skillet sailing through the air toward him in his *daed*'s moonlit kitchen. With equal deftness, he tossed aside his duffel bag and managed to catch the woman who was falling toward him too. Grabbing her around the waist, he pulled her protectively into his arms where she went limp, most likely too stunned to struggle to break free.

However, just to make sure there'd be no more flying objects, he gingerly removed the heavy frying pan from her grasp. He set it on the countertop out of her reach.

After steadying the woman on her feet, he kept his hold on her. He couldn't hide his amused smile as he stared into her wide-open eyes.

"I have to say, I've been wondering what kind of greeting I'd get after being gone from this house for five years. But this—" He choked back a chuckle. "It was like nothing I could've imagined." True, he hadn't been expecting any grand fanfare, but dodging a frying pan was totally unforeseen.

"You mean you're—" The woman gasped.

"Zach?" He nodded. "*Jah*, and I'm *verra*

sorry for scaring you. I'm guessing you might be Leah, my *daed*'s housekeeper and now his caregiver too. You're the one who contacted me?"

She answered with a nod.

"Nice to meet you. I think." He grinned, and cast a sideways glance at the skillet, trying to let her know he was teasing. But she didn't seem to be smiling.

"Um. You can let me go now."

"Oh, *jah*, right."

He loosened his grasp, and she slipped out of his arms, moving to turn on the kitchen light. Reddish-brown tendrils of hair had escaped from her *kapp*, but she didn't seem to notice or care.

"I didn't think you were coming." She bit her lip, almost looking more concerned than pleased that he had come. Which confused him.

"*Jah*, well, I can see why you'd think that. I've been in Michigan for a while and just got back to Indiana today and saw that you'd reached out to me. Right away, I hired an *Englisch* driver to bring me here, which is why I'm arriving so late." He rubbed his chin. "But I was thinking it wouldn't matter. I figured you'd be gone home by now and that *Daed* would be asleep. I thought I'd grab the key from under the flowerpot outside if I needed to."

"You were right about one of those things. Your *daed* is already—"

"Leah!" Mr. Graber called out from the bedroom, obviously awakened by their scuffle. "What's going on? Is that Matthew I hear?"

"Well, he *was* asleep," she said softly. "*Nee*, Mr. Graber." Her voice rose. "It's not Matthew."

She glanced up at him, and Zach knew she was waiting for him to answer on his own behalf. And rightfully so. But as he opened his mouth, he was surprised at how hesitant he felt. Over the years he'd grown to be a prominent and wealthy investor in Amish tourist properties in several states and had no trouble communicating with people. In fact, he thoroughly enjoyed those relationships and liked helping businesses and people in any way he could.

Yet suddenly the last words he'd heard from his father at age eighteen began taunting him, playing repeatedly in his mind. Painful, crushing words telling Zach that he wouldn't be readily forgiven for his foolhardy mistake. Those words had led him to pack up and move out of state. Now they made it hard for him to find his voice, until Leah urged him on with a nod.

"It's me, *Daed*," he finally said. "It's Zach."

"Zachary?" It didn't take half a brain to tell from his father's tone he was caught off guard.

"He didn't know you contacted me?" Zach whispered to Leah.

"I'm sorry, *nee*." Her eyes turned apologetic.

Hearing that, his heart instantly sank. Even though his father had never answered one of his letters over the years, he'd been encouraged by the message Leah had sent saying his help was much needed. Surely, he thought, this would be a time for his father to heal and for their relationship to do the same.

Now, realizing that his visit had nothing to do with his father's desire to see him, Zach slumped his shoulders and his body felt heavy with disappointment. The trip to Sugarcreek had been nearly three hundred miles, yet the walk to his father's bedroom seemed even longer. Leah went in ahead of him and turned on a lamp. The first thing he saw was his father's frown.

"I can't believe you're here," his *daed* croaked.

"Me either." Even though his father's tone wasn't the most welcoming, Zach tried to muster a grin. He also tried not to show his shock at seeing how much his father had changed. He'd had only specks of gray hair when Zach left and had been virile and strong. Now he was an aging man he barely recognized.

"Who told you to come? Matthew?"

Zach glanced at Leah. Seeing her strained expression, he worked around the question. "I heard about your accident through the Sugarcreek grapevine. I wanted to come, *Daed*."

"You did? Why? To see me hurting?"

Zach closed his eyes and inhaled deeply. Was there ever going to come a time when his father stopped thinking so poorly of him? Still, he held his tongue. What did his *mamm* used to say? Something about the right temperature at home is maintained by warm hearts, not hot heads?

"*Nee, Daed.* Just the opposite. I want to help out."

"Help, huh? You don't even like horses."

His father had always thought that of him. But nothing could've been further from the truth. What he didn't like, what had hurt, was all through his growing-up years how his father had put every minute of his time into training and doting on the creatures. It seemed his father's horses—not him or Matthew or even their mother on her deathbed—were his father's main concern, his pride and joy.

Yet, even given all Zach's own success, he still yearned for redemption. He longed to be Ivan Graber's trustworthy son.

"I like them enough to help," he answered honestly.

"Humph," his father snorted. "Are you staying at Matthew's?"

The question caused his head to jerk. "I, uh, I thought I'd stay here."

"That's up to Leah." His father immediately turned to his caregiver. "Is that *oll recht* with you? It'll mean extra work and more cooking."

"Of course, it's fine," Leah quickly replied. "The extra bedroom down the hall is clean as always and ready to sleep in. It will be no problem."

That resolved, his father shot him a stern look. "Leah's in charge. Don't you forget it."

"I won't," Zach replied solemnly, feeling belittled, like a grown man with a babysitter.

"*Oll recht*, I'm going back to sleep now. *Guti nacht.*"

His father rolled over in his bed, dismissing them. Even so, for a moment Zach stood frozen, praying that each day would get better not only in regard to his father's injuries, but in the discomfort that existed between the two of them. His heavenly plea ended when Leah turned off the lamp. Once more, he followed behind her. She spoke first when they reached the kitchen.

"That had to be hard on you."

"Only because I'd thought, well, I'd hoped…" He shook his head, resignedly. "It doesn't matter. I'm here to help in any way I can. I want what's best for *Daed*. And I can see he trusts you, which is a *gut* thing. He seems very fond of you."

"He's been a blessing to me as well."

Though he could hear the sincerity in the caregiver's raspy voice and see it in her doe-like hazel green eyes, that notion was hard to grasp.

"My daed?" He hadn't gotten many updates from his brother over the years, but when he did, Matthew typically mentioned an incident highlighting their father's ongoing obstinacy and brashness.

"Jah. I admit the first time *Grossmammi* had me take some leftovers to him I was in shock. Your *daed* grumbled at me for having to get up out of his chair and come to the door, which truly scared me." She chuckled. "It just took a while for me to get to know him better."

"Ah." He nodded, noncommittally, not knowing what to think about that.

"Well, I should go now." Leah picked up her tote.

"I'll walk you out," he offered.

After a few more words exchanged on the porch, he watched Leah make her way next door. Then he turned his eyes toward the end of the driveway. When he'd had the *Englisch* driver drop him off there so as not to cause any commotion with the horses, he'd been flooded with mixed emotions. Eyeing the Graber Horse Farm sign hanging crookedly on its post, Zach had felt like a stranger in a strange land—it was hard to feel any connection. Stalling, he'd reached out trying to right the cockeyed sign until he realized it would need more than a little help to set it straight. Zach hoped and prayed that wouldn't be true when it came to matters with his father. Apparently, though, things weren't going to be that easy.

Even so, he was here now, and may as well try his best. At least that's what he was figuring when he trudged inside to the "extra" bedroom assigned to him. The bedroom that long ago used to be his.

Chapter Two

Startled by a knock on her bedroom door, Leah shot up in bed and blinked at the morning sunshine beaming in her window.

"Leah, are you all right in there?" her cousin Catherine, who she fondly referred to as Cat, asked from outside the door.

Glancing at the clock on her nightstand, she saw it was way past her usual wake-up time. Hadn't the alarm gone off? Or had she slept right through it?

"Leah?" Her cousin sounded concerned.

"*Jah*, Cat, I'm fine. Just running late, it seems." Instantly, she threw back the sheet and jumped out of bed, heading for her closet.

"May I come in? I've got some *kaffe* for you."

"Oh, please do!"

Fortunately, it took no time to decide what

to wear. While Cat strode in and set a steaming mug on the dresser, Leah pulled her usual work uniform—a beige dress—from a hanger.

"*Danke* for the coffee, Cat, and for waking me up. I can't believe I overslept," she said in a rush as she slipped into her dress.

"Truth be told, I was worried. Usually it's you who's bringing me coffee before work."

"I know. Strange, *jah*?" She ran a quick brush through her hair and put it up in a knot. That done, she picked up the mug and rewarded herself with a few invigorating sips. "That was the best night of sleep I've had for weeks. I slept, really slept, for a change." Allowing herself a moment to reflect, she took a long swallow.

"I'm sure you needed it. You've been working seven days a week and long hours. I was in bed by the time you got home last night," her cousin noted. "Did you do something different at bedtime? Like drink some chamomile tea to relax you?"

Cupping the mug in her hands, Leah thought back to the previous night. Some of it had been stressful. Some of it pleasant, in an odd way. But all together, Zach Graber had seemed convincing that he'd come to help. Which felt promising and a relief. "I think I was feeling more at ease because Zach showed up."

"Zach?" All at once, Cat's eyes brightened in that way Leah knew to be pure captivation. "Zach Graber? He's here? How was it meeting him? Completely *wunderbaar*?"

"Completely embarrassing at first. I fell right into his arms."

"You?" Her cousin giggled. "Sensible, practical you? But then, Zach does have that effect on *maedels*," her cousin insisted. "Like I told you before, back in our younger years, every girl in Sugarcreek was smitten with him at one time or another. Why, if Thomas and I weren't a couple, I'd be vying for his attention right now."

"Believe me, there was no smittenness between us." She paused, wondering if that was a word. "In fact, I almost clobbered him with a skillet."

"You did what?"

Cat's mouth gaped. Meanwhile, Leah's cheeks heated, remembering. "You heard right."

With an amused grin, her cousin plopped down on the unmade bed. "I'm all ears, and I can be late getting to the bakery."

"Maybe you can. But I've got to get to work, Cat. I don't want Zach to think I'm slacking off just because he's here now."

"Oh, right." Her cousin jumped up. "You'll share soon, though?"

After Leah agreed, they both finished getting ready for work. She thought Cat was done with Zach talk until they walked out the front door about to go their separate ways.

"Didn't I tell you Zach has the dreamiest eyes? They were always sort of penetrating, like something you'd read about in a romance novel."

Leah didn't mention that her own eyes had been acting up in the past weeks, and that she couldn't have detected anything about Zach Graber's eyes even if she'd wanted to. This morning, however, she had already praised *Gott* that her vision was back to normal. Perhaps because of the good night's sleep she'd finally experienced? It had to be.

"I didn't notice. We talked some in the kitchen, then outside under the moonlight right before I left."

"That sounds even more romantic."

"Oh, Cat! Thomas sure has his hands full with you. *Gut* thing he knows that and loves you anyway."

"And you do too, cousin." Cat laughed as she skipped toward her bike.

Her cousin was right, of course. Leah had been so thankful when she'd inherited her grandmother's house and Cat had moved right in.

"Like a sister." Leah waved goodbye. "Be careful on the roads."

As Leah briskly took off across the yard, the sun was already plenty warm like any normal summer morning. What wasn't normal was the scene in Ivan's kitchen as she scurried inside.

Generally quiet and calm, the atmosphere was bright and lively. The undeniable aroma of homemade biscuits drifted beyond the oven door. A mason jar filled with daisies graced the table with a sweet innocence. And the originator of all those things was obviously an energetic Zach. Bent over the stove, he was humming while methodically stirring a skillet full of sausage gravy. His nearly six-foot frame was clad in an apron over his work clothes, which somehow didn't look silly on him at all.

"*Guder mariye!* You're just in time for breakfast." His cheerful greeting was accompanied by a broad smile that crinkled the corners of his deep blue eyes.

Once again, Leah stood transfixed, just as she had the night before. This time it wasn't from fear though. Rather, a man actually cooking?

"You know how to make biscuits and sausage gravy? Your *daed*'s favorites?" She said the first thing that came to mind.

"Doesn't everyone?"

"Not the men in my family. My brothers would starve to death if they had to fend for themselves in the kitchen."

"That's why I learned." He adjusted the burner and chuckled. "Starving is not the way I wish for the Lord to take me if I have anything to do with it."

Feeling nosy, she furtively inched closer, peering into the skillet. The consistency of the gravy looked perfect. Even better than her own.

"You do know I'm happy to do all the cooking just like I've always done."

"I figured you probably deserved a day off."

"Oh, you're making supper too?" She tilted her head and made it sound like she was jesting. But a part of her did wonder if he might be trying to take over things.

"*Nee*, I misspoke. Not supper too." He smiled. "I'm sure you've been managing just fine without me. I only started on breakfast because I didn't sleep that well and was up early."

He made the comment blithely, but true to her nature, she couldn't keep from reading more into it. While his arrival may have promised a bit of relief for her, she guessed that the strained reunion between father and son was going to make Zach's stay difficult.

"Well, your *daed* will be mighty happy with the breakfast you've made," she noted as she watched him remove a baking sheet of perfectly formed biscuits from the oven.

Setting the sheet on a trivet, he laid aside the pot holder and turned to her. He ruffled a hand through his light brown hair. "If you don't mind, can we act like you made breakfast?"

"After you went to all this trouble?"

"I think it would be best. I don't want *Daed* thinking I'm trying to take over or outshine you. Not that I'm saying I could. But who knows?" He shed the apron, tossing it over a kitchen chair. "He may be afraid to eat, thinking I'm trying to poison him."

His comment caused her to blink. "Are you teasing or serious?"

"A little of both, I guess. I haven't been around him for years. He may be skittish about me. You saw for yourself last night. It's going to take some time to get back on solid ground with him."

In truth, she could appreciate that. Ever since Zach had arrived, hadn't she been sizing him up in her own way? "Well, if that's what you think is best."

"*Jah*, I do."

She was shocked at how her heart went out to him, but it involuntarily did. Also, she couldn't help thinking of Mr. Graber. Wouldn't he find more peace by making things right with his son? Again, she had to remind herself whatever their issue was, it wasn't hers to solve.

"Then I won't say a word about it when I take his breakfast tray to him," she promised.

As they worked together filling up the tray with biscuits and gravy, a cup of fruit, orange juice and coffee, she could sense Zach was trying to get a handle on his *daed*'s condition.

"Isn't *Daed* able to come to the kitchen to eat?" he asked.

"According to the doctor, he's allowed to. Maybe not so comfortably or painlessly with the crutches and his other injuries. But he could if he wanted to. I've offered to help him, of course, and it's not a far way to go, as you know." She sighed. "It just seems like he'd rather spend time alone in his room. At first, I would keep him company and eat in there with him. But then, I stopped because I felt like it was doing him more harm than good."

"And now, maybe he won't want to come into the kitchen because I'm here."

"At least you know the behavior didn't start with you," she offered as she picked up the tray. "I'll let your *daed* know that I'm taking you around the property after breakfast so I can show you what work needs to be done."

"*Jah*, he won't mind if he knows you're the boss and that the orders are coming from you."

His comment made Leah wonder if Zach minded. But if he did, it didn't show.

"In the meantime, may I set a place for you at the table?" He arched a brow.

"Of course." She glanced down at the tray in her hands. "My mouth's been watering, smelling all of this. Thank you for making it."

"It was easy as pie."

"Oh, you make pies as well?"

He chuckled. "That's just an expression as I'm sure you know."

"I do know. I'm glad now that I didn't crash that skillet over your head last night."

"Because you would've missed out on biscuits and gravy?"

"Exactly." She laughed, then headed for the bedroom.

Ivan's face lit up as soon as he saw the tray and got a whiff of his favorite breakfast. She couldn't blame him. She was looking forward to breakfast, too, and to getting a new day started. A new, productive day that could possibly lead to their old routines.

"I'd add this to the list too." Zach wiggled the top of the crooked wooden gate that had visibly come loose from its post. "It looks like it's missing a—"

"Missing hinge on gate, south side meadow,"

Leah said as she scribbled on her notepad. "Got it."

After breakfast, when Zach followed Leah's lead in checking out maintenance issues around his father's property, he thought she was going overboard by bringing along a pad of paper and pencil. He'd already made a mental note of the buckling porch steps he'd tripped on as well as the barely hanging Graber Horse Farm sign. He assumed his brain was large enough to store a few more items that needed fixing.

But now that they'd been walking the grounds for a half hour and still had a way to go, he was glad Leah had been so efficient. So far, she was on page three of necessary repairs.

"Where to next?" Knowing Leah was currently more familiar with his father's place, Zach was happy for her guidance.

"Do you mind if we head down to the creek?" Leah asked. "When you were talking about cleaning out the overgrown trenches along the driveway in case of heavy rains, it reminded me of another possible problem."

"Considering how the day's heating up so quickly—" Zach squinted into the sun "—the creek sounds like a good choice."

This time, rather than Leah leading, they walked side by side. Once again he noticed that, just like at breakfast, she had a way of making conversation easy and situations comfortable.

"The list got mighty long quickly, didn't it? I'm sorry for that."

"Nothing for you to be sorry about. I'm fine doing the work. But it's hard to believe that *Daed*'s property has been going downhill just since the accident."

"I think if everything simply gets fixed and back in place, he'll be in a good spot again," she replied confidently. "And if you need assistance with these repairs, if I can be of help, I'll have you know I'm not afraid to get my hands dirty."

"Oh, now that's something that I *can* believe."

She gave him a curious look.

"Not that you appear to be messy or anything." He backtracked. "What I mean is, you seem like a person who's willing to do whatever it takes to get a job done."

Her cheeks seemed to turn rosier at that. "I don't know. I just try to do the right thing, I guess."

As they strolled down the slope of grass that led to the creek, she seemed almost relieved to steer his attention from her to the existing problem there. The waterway was as picturesque as he'd remembered it, lush with cattail plants and wildflowers on one side of the stream and a grouping of shade trees on the other. However, a large ash tree had uprooted, landing across the middle of the creek bed.

"I saw the tree when I came down here a few weeks ago to relax and read." Leah looked up at him. "If rains get heavy like you mentioned before, could the trunk dam up the creek and cause any problems?"

"You know, I'm not sure," he admitted. "But let's add it to the list, and I'll get it sawed into pieces and moved. Even if it's not a problem, it'd be fun to bring Matthew's boys down here to romp in the water like he and I used to do. They're so little, they'd never get over this trunk."

"That would be nice for them." She jotted on her pad, smiling. "You and Matthew played down here?"

"And neighbor kids too."

He started to tell her he even got his first kiss on the cheek here when he was eight years old. Only because it was a funny event when Sarah Speicher had lost a game that they were all playing, and the kiss was her punishment so to speak. But for sure he didn't know Leah well enough to be telling her such a thing. Or how he and Sarah had kissed plenty more times by the same creek ten years later. Right before he fled to Indiana without even saying goodbye to her. He pushed away that memory as well as the thought that he hadn't been involved with another woman since.

"I'm sure it was a *gut* place to play." A joyful glint shone in Leah's eyes.

"It was." He worked to get his mind refocused on the present. "So, are we finished with the list?"

"You probably wish we were." She winced. "But we haven't been to the horse barn yet." Looking intent, she began to trudge up the bank. He followed right beside her.

"But remember? I told you at breakfast that I'd already fed the horses before I started in the kitchen this morning. Once I finished making the rounds with you, I planned to let them out and muck the stalls. So, if you want to head back to the house, I can do that on my own."

She acted like she hadn't heard that last part, and continued walking in the direction of the barn. "I do remember. You said your favorite mare Sugar was happier to see you than your *daed* was."

Obviously, she'd heard that right.

In minutes, they were about to pass the house along their way. But instead of Leah slipping inside and attending to her work there, she kept in step alongside him all the way to the barn. When he had to open the door by gripping its edge due to a broken handle, she readily made a note of it without him having to say a word.

The moment they entered the barn, the un-broken horse stalled on the right side greeted them with squeals, pawing at the floor. "He reacted the same way when I stopped in earlier," Zach reported. "He's not happy with me."

"Don't take it personally. I think he misses his friend, meaning the horse that threw your *daed*. We exchanged this horse for the other one. But with taking care of your *daed*, I haven't had a chance to spend any time with him."

Pencil to paper, she began writing. He glanced around, trying to detect what she'd seen that needed repairs and couldn't come up with anything. He was about to ask her what she'd written when she glanced up at him with a sorry expression. "I will say, you're going to have your hands full training this unruly creature."

His hands immediately shot up in the air. "I'm going to what? *Nee*. You need to erase that."

He didn't know how her hazel green eyes could display any more emotion, but as she pleaded, they did. "But your dad spent money on him, and it's going to be a while before he can get to training him. And he needs that to happen so he can sell the horse and make money on it."

Over and over, Zach shook his head. "I'm sorry about that. But training a horse can't be on the list because it's not on my list of skills."

Her instantaneous chuckle seemed to be a mixture of pure amusement and utter disbelief. "Do you mean to say that you know how to make a *wunderbaar* breakfast, but you don't know the first thing about breaking a horse? After you lived with a father who trained horses all his life?"

He had been taking a liking to her raspy voice, finding it interesting. But now it was heightened to an unpleasant pitch.

"I only know how to feed them and clean up after them. Growing up, that's all Matthew and I did for my father. It's all he instructed us to do. Besides, I'm not planning to be in Sugarcreek long enough to train a horse."

Her mouth immediately curved downward. He knew her look of disappointment had nothing to do with him leaving. Just him leaving without getting the training done.

"Well…" She let out a long sigh. "While you are here, could you at least make him more comfortable in his new setting? Then he won't be such a noisy nuisance for Sugar and Star and the other horses that are long-term residents and needed around the farm. He'd also be more trainable when your *daed* is ready to take on the job again. Could you do that for him?" Her brows creased and her mouth pouted.

"Um…" It was his turn to exhale heavily.

"Please?"

How could he say no to her after all she'd been doing? "*Oll recht*, I'll try to get him feeling more at home."

"Oh, *gut*!" She glanced heavenward as if giving thanks. "I'm guessing you know how important it is to first build a bond of trust with an animal."

"Of course. That's part of any relationship, ain't so?"

"*Jah*, and trust ain't easily attained. But it sure is easily broken." The way she spoke, he had to wonder if she was talking from experience. "And I've read that with horses there are three steps involved in building that bond," she continued. "Do you want to know what they are?"

"Besides feeding them, grazing them and cleaning up after them?" he asked.

It took her a moment to realize he was making a joke. She giggled before launching into an explanation of what she'd read and studied.

Meanwhile, he latched his hands on to his suspenders, musing more than listening. In less than twenty-four hours since his arrival, between his father and the farm and now the untamed horse, there was already more fixing to do than he would've ever envisioned. And while he appreciated Leah's positive nature, again, he knew there was no way his father's place had fallen apart in only a matter of weeks. Also, after seeing his father's physical decline, he couldn't imagine how his *daed* could go on maintaining everything. None of it made good business sense, and being the businessman that he'd grown to be…

Suddenly, it came to him. A way that he could provide a secure future for his father.

"I'll take that list from you," he said to Leah as soon as she'd finished her explanation.

She ripped the pages from the tablet and handed them to him. He gripped the papers like a lifeline.

"So, you're up for taking the first step with the new horse then?" she asked.

"You mean…" he hedged, flipping through the pages, hoping she'd fill in the blank about what that initial step might be.

"Spending time with him."

"Uh, sure. Not a problem." He smiled at her. Given a little time—and plenty of handy work—his plan could work out. Hopefully, his brother would agree.

Chapter Three

~❧

Leah half wished she could spend her entire Saturday the way she used to before Mr. Graber's accident: catching up on her own housecleaning, laundry and yard work. But in the past few days, since she and Zach had put together the lengthy maintenance list, Zach had been working nonstop. Which meant she needed to continue to do her part, too, in the effort to get Ivan Graber's life back to normal.

After a few quick swipes to dust her furniture and just as fast of a sweeping of her kitchen floor, she put away her dust cloth and broom. Already later than usual, she picked up her quilted bag and headed next door.

Right away, she spotted Zach bent over his father's porch steps with a canvas tool-apron wrapped around his waist and a hammer in his hands. The sun shone brightly on him almost like a spotlight. It also highlighted his work.

"Zach, the porch steps! They look *wunderbaar*!" She couldn't contain her astonishment. "The job you're doing, why, it's amazing!"

Zach stood up, giving her a curious smile. "You're getting mighty excited about steps, ain't so?" He chuckled.

"I can't help it. They're all smooth and even."

"Like steps should be?"

"*Jah*, and they make the house look fresher, don't you think?"

"Honestly…" He ran a hand over the porch railing. "I was thinking the opposite. Now I feel like I should repaint the railing and shutters, so they look new too."

She hadn't noticed the chipped white paint on those areas until then. "I see what you mean. Well, still, you should feel good about all you've gotten done so far. I saw you outside earlier, too, spending time with the untamed horse."

"You mean Bear? That's what I named him. It seemed a match for his overbearing personality and dark color. I managed to get him on a lead rope and do a little walking like you suggested."

"Did he like it?"

"I'm not sure. I was too nervous about me to worry about him. When I did get brave enough to look him in the eye, he seemed to be sizing me up."

"They'll do that." She laughed. "And how's your *daed* this morning?" Inwardly, she chided herself. She hadn't meant to segue from one strained relationship to another.

"He was happy with the pancakes I served, but not so thrilled to see me instead of you."

"I'm sorry I didn't get here earlier to help."

"I'm surprised to see you here at all. I thought I told you to take the day off to catch up on your own chores."

"They'll wait. Your *daed*'s concerns are way more important."

"I hope you're getting paid extra for the weekends then."

She didn't bother to mention she was taking less than her weekly rate no matter how many hours she worked. Once again, she truly believed the time would come soon when everything, including finances, would be back to normal.

"So…what haven't you accomplished since dawn?" She was beginning to feel guilty.

"Well." He paused to wipe a sweaty brow. "I wasn't able to get *Daed* up and into the kitchen."

"He didn't give in to your nudging either, huh?" She sighed. "Well, we'll have to keep working on him about that," she said, realizing that was going to take as much work as the farm repairs. "I was about to go inside and see if there's anything special he wants from the grocery before I head out." At least there was still money set aside in a drawer for food, thankfully. "Sometimes he gets a taste for something he wants me to make."

"I'm planning to go into town too. I'd like to drop in on Matthew's family since I haven't seen them yet. I'll, uh, be finished here soon if you want to go together." He squinted, arching an inviting brow. "No sense in taking two buggies. That is, if you think *Daed* can be left alone while he's awake," he added quickly.

"I've had to run into town a few times before you arrived, and he didn't seem to have a problem with it. I almost think he liked me being gone for a little while, so I wasn't hovering as much."

"Then we'll leave in just a bit," Zach replied.

Twenty minutes later, as Zach steered the buggy along the country road, Leah had to admit it felt mighty good to be getting away from the house for a short time. Seeing people on the roadside and out in their yards reminded her that life did still exist beyond the Graber farm. Absorbing the sights of bright-colored gardens and plentiful crops along the way was refreshing as well.

"It's pretty country, isn't it?" Zach glanced from side to side, appearing as pleased as she was to be taking in the scenery.

"*Jah*, makes a person feel at peace." She sighed wistfully as they clip-clopped past yet another fenced-in property, where horses dotted a meadow, lazily grazing. That reminded her of something.

"When we pulled out of your *daed*'s place, I noticed you'd already fixed the Graber Horse Farm sign."

"It wasn't too difficult. Not like the hard work you do each day, taking care of my father. You're *wunderbaar* at what you do, Leah."

She could feel her cheeks turn pink, reason enough to shift focus back to him. "How did you learn to fix so many things?"

"Somehow it always came naturally to me," he answered without a hint of pride in his voice. "I liked to study whatever thing was broken and tinker around till I got it working. Even as a young boy my *mamm* called me Mr. Fixit."

"Is that what you do in Indiana? Fix things?"

"In a way," he answered vaguely. "What

about you? Have you always enjoyed taking care of people?"

His question made her stop and reflect in a manner she never had before. "I suppose I could say in a way too. I guess I always felt I should look for a means to make someone feel better, happier. But as a young girl, a lot of times that was by reading to a person." She started to mention how she used to read to her little brother but stopped herself. There was no need to delve into that sad story. "I feel reading is a way people can get to know more about *Gott* and the world He created for us. The animals, plants, people, emotions, His Word."

"I have seen a lot more books around *Daed*'s house than before. Those from you?"

"I keep thinking he might pick one up and read it."

"That could be a first. My *mamm* is the one who always read to us. Even any Bible reading came from her. She had a sweet voice."

It was easy to see how Zach's expression softened as he spoke of his mother. "It's been five years now since she went to be with the Lord," he added.

It wasn't lost on her that it was the same number of years that Zach had been gone from Sugarcreek. But when she looked over to see if he was going to share more about what had caused him to leave back then, he was gazing out the left side of the buggy. And she wasn't about to pry.

"It's been around two years since my parents have both been gone," she said. "But I feel blessed to have had them that long since they didn't have me until they were older in life. It was also a blessing to have some time to spend with my *grossmammi.*"

"I didn't know your parents." He offered a sincere glance. "But your grandmother was a special lady, and you have my sympathy. What a kind woman she was, always thinking of others. It seems you've taken after her."

"Oh, I don't know about that." She flushed, shifting in her seat. "But I do agree she was *verra* special." Without a doubt, a little over a year ago when she learned that her maternal grandmother here in northern Ohio needed assistance, the timing couldn't have been more perfect for her to move from West Union. It had been a blessing to have a reason to escape the betrayal she'd been dealt by her older siblings and ex-fiancé. The grandmother she'd never really known before had been a salve to her hurting heart. She was loving and appreciative of Leah even till her last breath.

"She used to make Matthew and me the best chocolate chip cake. It was even better than our *mamm*'s cakes." He smiled. "But we never said so."

He laughed and Leah joined in. "I still have her recipe. I'll have to bake one soon."

"I sure wouldn't mind if you did." His lips curved upward.

They talked easily during the rest of the ride into town. As Zach dropped her off at the grocery, he promised to be back within the hour.

Pushing her cart up and down the grocery aisles, she was glad to be taking her time. She paused momentarily at an endcap display of eyeglasses. But since her vision had seemed fine the past couple of days, she kept moving.

Until she got to the baking aisle.

Stopping in front of the bags of chocolate chips, she took more than a minute, deciding whether to buy some. Finally, she tossed a bag into her cart. Ivan liked any sweets she made, especially ones with chocolate. And Zach... His open smile and sweet words about her grandmother ran across her mind. So did the fact that it had been a long while since she'd baked something special for a man her own age. The mere idea of it caused her cheeks to flush. But immediately she shook her head to dismiss the feeling, determined to keep such thoughts in check. Besides, there were plenty of other things to be concerned with and to keep her busy these days. One of which was everything still left on her grocery list.

Sometimes Zach wished it wasn't second nature for him to see a piece of property and notice its imperfections right away. Which is what he found himself doing even before he hitched Sugar to a post outside Matthew's house. Forcing himself to look away from the few items that needed fixing, he worked to concentrate on the peacefulness of his brother's one-acre surroundings. Like the weeping willow tree rustling softly in the whispering breeze. The two cats curled up together on the porch. And the pleasant tinkling sound of a wind chime.

Taking it all in, he was happy that his brother's family had such a blissful place to live. He was ready to tell that to Matthew, too, when he knocked on the door, and his brother opened it.

"Matthew, your new place is—"

"Samuel! Jonah! Be careful what you're doing!"

Zach's nephews didn't appear to be doing much listening to their father, unlike their baby sister cuddled in Matthew's arms who began wailing the moment she heard her father shout. The five-and three-year-old boys shot out the door with their arms spread like wings, almost knocking into Zach. Making sounds like—well, he wasn't sure what they were imitating. Whatever it was, in a millisecond they managed to undo the tranquil atmosphere.

"They're pretending to be hawks they've seen," Matthew spoke up over the din as he stepped out onto the porch and the boys continued circling them.

"I didn't realize Sugarcreek hawks sounded like that." Zach laughed, watching the boys reroute their flights out into the yard.

"Oh, *jah*. You wouldn't believe the noise Sugarcreek's human hawks can make." Matthew bounced up and down, trying to shush his daughter. "Anyway, *willkumme* back, *bruder*. It's *gut* to see you. I'd give you a better greeting, but—"

"I'd say your hands are full with this little beauty. Hi, Lydia. Nice to meet you. I'm your *onkel*." Zach ventured to soothe the baby by gently running the back of his hand along her cheek. However, that only incited more crying.

"I hope you're not losing your touch with females," Matthew's *frau* clucked teasingly as she walked out the front door. Apparently, Anna had witnessed his failed attempt. "Haven't you been getting enough practice?"

Growing up, he'd always been fond of Anna and was glad his brother had made such a wonderful woman his wife. "I suppose I need to work on that."

"Well, I can help, for sure. It *is* about time you settled down. Don't you think?" Her questioning eyes twinkled at him.

"Anna, you're *verra* kind. But aren't you rushing things? I've hardly been back in town any time at all, and already you're trying to find me a wife?" Zach grinned at his sister-in-law.

"Or even a longtime crush on someone." She smiled up at him. "Anything to get you to return to Sugarcreek for good. I thought that might be your plan last year when I read one of your letters to Matthew. Why, I even told some friends you were moving back."

"You did what?" Zach blinked. "I never said that."

However, he could easily recall the letter Anna was referring to. In it, he'd gotten carried away with memories of happier times in Sugarcreek flowing from his pen. But that was only because he did have a soft spot for the town that he'd grown up in. Yet he never intended to settle here for good.

"Well, we'll see how things go." Anna winked. "Maybe you won't make a liar out of me yet."

He was pretty sure he would, but he left that

unsaid as he watched her remove the sobbing *boppli* from Matthew's arms.

"It's time for her bottle. Boys!" she called out. "Come give your *Onkel* Zach a hug. Then go inside for a snack while I feed your sister. Your dad and uncle need a few minutes' peace to catch up."

Anna seemed to have a better grip on the boys than his brother. Right away the boys heeded her words. His heart warmed as he bent down to receive their hugs, which were quick but sweet. After that, Anna ushered the children indoors, but not before promising Zach a future family dinner, and a lunch for Matthew to take to work.

"How's your new position going?" Zach had noticed his brother looked tired. Why wouldn't he with all he had going on? "Are you getting settled in?"

"Being promoted to manager is *wunderbaar*. I like the work and appreciate the opportunity. But when something goes wrong, I'm the one who needs to oversee the problem. And you can be sure something's always going wrong." His voice rose emphatically. "Yesterday, I put in a twelve-hour day. And today, I'm supposed to be off, but…"

"You have to go into work."

Matthew nodded. "I feel bad because Anna's doing more than she should lately. But you know her. She takes it all in stride. And, as much as I want to help at *Daed*'s, Zach, I can't seem to find the time right now. I don't know when I ever can, honestly. And I'm real thankful you came to help, but I'm guessing you can't stay forever. You'll be wanting to get back to Indiana, *jah*?"

"That's my plan when things get settled here."

"You know, I've never been sure exactly what you do." His brother gave him a curious frown. "I know you started out in Shipshewana renovating homes and then some investor came along, and you started flipping houses together. That's the term, right?"

"It is."

"And then after that, you—I'm not sure what you did."

His brother didn't know because Zach had never shared how he'd used the profits from those house sales to become a silent investor in Amish tourist properties. He'd found Amish business owners were pleased to be in a financial relationship with other Amish folks. And although in his role he wasn't involved in the daily operations of those businesses, he was humbled and grateful to *Gott* any time that he could be of assistance to them. Truth be told, his investments had paid off so handsomely he could purchase his father's property a dozen times and still have plenty of money in the bank. Even so, he hadn't come to Sugarcreek to outdo his father. He'd come for his *daed*.

"Sometimes I'm not sure either," Zach jested, aiming to divert Matthew from the subject. "The thing is, we're both busy, but that doesn't mean we don't want to help our father. I'm just not sure that only patching things up for him is what's best for his future."

"Speaking of patching up things, how was it seeing *Daed*?"

On the few occasions that Zach had the opportunity to come to Sugarcreek on business, he'd dropped in at Matthew and Anna's. Yet he'd promised himself he'd never intrude on his father until the day his father sought him out. Which was exactly what had happened this time—at least he'd thought so. The disappointing reminder caused Zach to draw in a deep breath.

"I guess if I hadn't been hoping for the best, it wouldn't have seemed like the worst. He doesn't seem pleased about me being here. But even if I can't change that, I'd like to try to change things for him for the better. I'm telling you, Matthew, yesterday when I saw how run-down *Daed*'s entire place is, I could tell it hasn't been just since the accident that the farm has been going downhill."

"I agree. So what are you thinking?" Matthew crossed his arms, and leaned against the porch railing, looking eager to listen.

"I'd say the first step is to get the farm back into tip-top shape. It'll take a few weeks, but I can do that," Zach assured him. "Then, instead of putting it up for sale, given the location of the farm, I'm thinking I'd like to call on some business contacts I've made over the years—property developers and business owners. I even may be able to get in touch with a prestigious racehorse trainer I know of." He didn't mention that the trainer Caleb King, back in Indiana, had offered to take care of Zach's horse for as long as he'd be in Sugarcreek. "I can't help but think one of those people would be interested in buying *Daed*'s property," he added.

"How do you know people like them?"

"How do you know what you do about the brick-making industry? You just do," he answered vaguely, then waited on his brother's reaction. He felt a wave of relief when Matthew's eyes lit up.

"It's a blessing for *Daed* that you have those kinds of connections. And just think. When you get his place in shape and use your contacts to get a great price for it and secure a future for him, there's nothing he can complain about you then."

"Well, I don't know about that." Zach prayed with his entire being that his father would feel that way. But even if his father never did, at least Zach would've tried to express his love by doing the best he could for him. "*Daed* may have aged, but he's still stubborn and spirited."

"No doubt, but unbroken horses are that way too," his brother countered. "And training them is a majorly physical job. Whether *Daed* will admit it or not, I don't think it's a job he can still manage to do. No wonder he got hurt. And his money must be dwindling. He hasn't been training as many horses as he used to."

"If everything goes as I'm thinking it can, there'd be no strain on his health or his pocketbook anymore."

"I think it's a great plan, Zach."

"I'm really glad you do. So…" He paused. "I know you've got lots on your plate, Matthew, but could you set aside an hour? Just so we can sit down together with *Daed* and explain what I'm proposing to do?"

His brother's sleep-deprived eyes shot wide open. "Zach, you can't be serious. If you tell him—even if I tell him—if it's coming from us, he'll say no right away."

Taking a moment to imagine the scene, Zach could feel his jaw tighten. His brother was probably right. "*Oll recht.* I'll get everything back in shape, and I'll start reaching out to my contacts. We'll go from there to find a way to make things work for everyone."

His brother's shoulders slackened. He appeared more relaxed. "Thank you, Zach. Truly, *danke.*"

"You've been keeping a watch on our father for a long time, Matthew. It's the least I can do." Thinking of the other person in their father's life, he smiled. "I'll let Leah know that you and I talked and what we're planning."

"Ahh... I wouldn't be so fast to do that either."

"*Nee?*" Zach was puzzled.

"She may slip up and tell *Daed.* Like we just said, that wouldn't be such a good idea until there's a definite plan or offers on his property. Also, I doubt she'd feel comfortable keeping our plans from him."

"I can see that about her for sure. I mean about her not wanting to be secretive. All right," he said, as decisively as he could manage. "Leah wants to see things improve for *Daed*, so we're all thinking along the same line in that respect."

"And that will take a while to do. So, until then…"

Matthew's voice trailed off in conclusion. However, Zach's thoughts didn't dwindle one bit after saying goodbye to his brother. As he rode to pick up Leah from the grocery, he continued mulling over everything Matthew had said. Once again, he had to admit his brother was probably right. Their father was their responsibility, not Leah's. As kind a person as she was, she shouldn't have to feel pressured to make their father's future her life's work. Why, she was already doing enough, he thought, as he pulled up to the store and saw her waiting for him with a full cart.

"How was your visit with Matthew's family?" she asked once they got the groceries packed in the buggy and she slipped in beside him.

"Really good. I got to see him and Anna and sweet little Lydia. And my nephews too, of course, who are hoots."

She chuckled. "I'm sure it's fun for Anna and your brother but a lot of work too. I know Matthew was feeling badly that he couldn't be of more help. But I hope he knows now that you and I can work together to get things back to the way they were for your *daed*. Ain't so?"

She looked over at him with a reassuring

smile, and he nodded in agreement. As he did, a twinge of guilt poked at him. He had a feeling if he even hinted about what he and Matthew had talked about, Leah would be put off. She'd be eyeing him just as skeptically as Bear had earlier that morning. He surely didn't want Leah to be mad at him, but he also didn't want to look too closely at the reason why.

Chapter Four

Leah wasn't at all hesitant when Zach asked if they could make a quick stop before leaving town. She felt guilty admitting it to herself, but she wasn't in a major rush to get back to the farm. She was enjoying watching Amish families and *Englischers* stroll along the sidewalks. And she had no worries that any groceries would go bad or melt in a matter of minutes.

"I'd like to check out something for *Daed* in the Med-Mart Supplies shop," Zach explained as he pulled into the store's parking lot.

"What are you thinking of getting?" she asked.

"I want to see if they have a knee scooter. They come in handy for a person with an ankle cast. It's not like riding a horse, of course." He gave a wan smile. "But it may be more to his liking. With his aching ribs and wrist, it could be easier on him than the crutches."

"Oh, that's a great idea. Sugar and I will be happy to wait for you."

As Zach hopped down from the buggy and hitched Sugar to the post, Leah felt hopeful. A scooter could be just the thing to get Ivan back on his feet, and she was thankful Zach had thought of it. But then, from everything she'd witnessed so far, Zach did seem to be a thoughtful man, looking for ways to help his father. Which left her stunned a moment later when she heard someone greet him loudly and somewhat sarcastically as he made his way over to the sidewalk.

"Why, if it isn't Zachary! The Graber black sheep."

Beyond curious, she inched over to Zach's side of the buggy to get a better look at the man addressing him. The person appeared to be about the same age as Zach, though far stockier.

Seemingly caught off guard, Zach swayed slightly before digging in his heels. "Grabers don't deal in sheep, Uri, only horses. You know that."

"And did *you* know my sister Sarah, who you abandoned, is happily married with three *kinner*?"

Abandoned? Zach, who she'd just decided was caring and considerate, had deserted a woman?

Whatever the situation had been with the girl, she noticed Zach shifted uneasily on his feet.

"That's wonderful news," he said. "Please tell Sarah I'm happy for her."

"No need for me to do that." The man's expression turned snarly. "Sarah's happy enough on her own without your sentiments."

"Again, that's *gut* to hear, Uri. Take care."

Zach started to walk around him, but the burly man made a point of leaning in and knocking Zach's shoulder as Zach passed by. She could see Zach's hands rapidly tighten into fists by his sides, but he loosened them just as quickly before ducking into the shop.

She hadn't realized she'd been holding her breath, praying the two men wouldn't get into a row. Until Uri finally walked away, and she let out an audible sigh. Apparently so loud that Sugar turned to look at her.

"Oh, Sugar, did you see that? That was mighty scary. Do you know the Sarah they were talking about?"

Of course, she wasn't expecting an answer. She also wasn't expecting her past in West Union to suddenly show its face in the present. But the talk of abandonment instantly brought her ex-fiancé Aaron Yoder to mind. In all the years they had courted, how had she let herself be so fooled by the kind of man he really was?

Upon hearing the entire story, Cat had said that Aaron had done Leah a favor.

But, was *Gott* ever going to bring the right person into her life? She sighed again, although more quietly this time. Then, forcing herself to sit up straight and look beyond herself, she began people watching again. Soon Zach came out of the shop, carrying a collapsible scooter in his arms. He looked pleased and at ease, as if the uncomfortable conversation with Sarah's brother had never happened.

"I rented the scooter for two months," he told her as he placed it in the back seat of the buggy. "But I can pay for additional weeks if *Daed* needs it."

"I really think your *daed* will like it, Zach."

"I sure hope so," he replied as he went to unhitch Sugar.

Once they made their way through the main street of town and Zach steered the buggy onto the winding country road, Leah surreptitiously glanced at him. Already it felt comfortable to be sitting alongside the man from Indiana. Which, in a way, was strange and disturbing. After all, should she be trusting him? She'd just experienced proof that they didn't know much of each other's history. But then, should that even matter?

Oddly enough, they seemed to be getting along easily now. Which most likely had everything to do with having Ivan's well-being as their common goal. Admittedly, she was thankful that he'd come to Sugarcreek and that they were climbing the proverbial mountain named Ivan together.

As soon as they arrived at the farm, it didn't take much time to unload the groceries and for Zach to retrieve the scooter. Setting it aside, he politely began to help put away groceries. That is, until Leah placed a hand on his arm to stop him.

"Zach, I can do that later. I'm too excited about the scooter to wait."

"*Gut* to hear. I am too." He smiled. "But I think you should take the scooter into the bedroom for *Daed.*"

"*Nee*, Zach. Not again. That's just like the morning you made your *daed*'s favorite breakfast and had me take the credit for it."

"I know. But since you're his caregiver, I believe you'll get better results than me. And that's what's important. Right?"

Once more, she reluctantly bowed to his wishes. In an instant, he set up the scooter and showed her how it worked. More than excited, she wheeled it into Ivan's bedroom with Zach following behind her. She couldn't stop giggling, thinking it was the most fun she'd had in a while.

The sound of her laughter appeared to rouse Ivan. He sat up a little straighter on his bed that she'd made earlier, and a slight smile crept onto his lips.

"We're back from town, Mr. Graber, and look what we brought for you. It's a knee scooter. You just put your casted ankle up here and use your good leg to get around. It's kind of fun."

"Oh, *jah*?" His eyes lit up some. "Where did you get it?"

"Zach rented it from Med-Mart." His name accidentally slipped out.

"You say Zach did that?" Ivan's delighted expression immediately dimmed.

"*Jah.* Wasn't that thoughtful of him?"

The man was silent.

"Wasn't it, Mr. Graber?" She felt her jaw clench.

He lifted a hand and, at first, she thought he might be ready to get up and try it. But he pointed to a corner on the far side of the room. "You can put it over there."

"*Ach!*" She'd never had a mule but if they truly were as stubborn as the man that she took care of, she felt sorry for anyone who owned one. "Mr. Graber..." She worked to gather her patience. "I know you're uncomfortable and still in pain but lying in bed isn't helping. You need to start getting up and about, and the scooter will help you do that."

She glanced at Zach, hoping he might chime in. Instead every glimmer of hope that had shone in his face had vanished. "I'll put it over there out of the way," he said quietly.

"Okay. Well..." She let out an exasperated breath. "I'll put the groceries away and then make lunch for everyone."

Like a petulant child, Ivan crossed his arms over his chest. "I'm not hungry."

"But you're always hungry."

"And I have lots of work waiting for me," Zach declared.

"You always have work waiting for you."

Hands on her hips, she looked back and forth between the two of them only to see Ivan shrug. Then Zach shrugged in the exact same manner. There was no denying the pair were related.

"All right then." She clasped her hands together. "*Danke* for making things so easy for me. I'll make lunch for me and only me, and supper will be ready by six. Surely you both will be ready to eat by then."

With that, she stomped off to the kitchen and

started emptying the grocery bags. After Zach stored the scooter, he came out of his father's bedroom, heading for the back door. Glancing at him, she could see disappointment shadowing his face. After knowing how glad he'd looked leaving the medical supply shop just a half hour earlier, her heart went out to him. So much so that she couldn't let him just walk out.

"Here." She picked two apples and a banana from the fruit bowl on the counter and approached him. "For the horses...or for you if you get hungry."

"Danke." He paused, twirling one of the apples in the palm of his hand. She thought he was about to say something, but then he seemed to change his mind. He was halfway out the screen door when she spoke up.

"Zach."

He turned to look at her.

"You tried."

He raised and lowered those strong-looking shoulders of his in response again.

This time she couldn't blame him for his shrug. She felt the same way.

Zach had put in a long, exhausting day when he hoisted himself up on the fence overlooking the pasture, taking a moment's rest. Happy to remove his hat, he set it atop the fence post, then swiped a dust-covered forearm across his sweaty brow.

After spending hour after hour in the burning sun doing yard work, it did feel good knowing he could cross a few items off the job list. He'd sawed the fallen tree overlying the creek and chopped it into firewood. The trenches along the driveway were now free of overgrowth and flushed out. He'd also trimmed a few bushes and cut down dead tree limbs.

Yet, for all his labor, he knew he'd barely made a dent in all that needed to be done. It was more proof that there was no way his father could physically manage the demands of the place anymore. And his father for sure wasn't making enough money to hire help to do the job.

Zach stared out into the meadow and couldn't help but think that even as pretty and peaceful as it was, the pastureland was also filled with its own kind of work. Controlling weeds, reseeding and improving soil were on the short list. Not to mention taking care of the animals that grazed on that plot of land.

Trying to still his thoughts, he gazed into the sky.

Heavenly Father, I know You're always looking upon us. So I'm asking—help me please to find the right people, the right cir-

cumstance, that will benefit my father at this time in his life. Something that he'll be pleased with. Something he'll accept way better than my scooter idea!

He was still thinking about the earlier episode with his father and feeling bruised by his *daed*'s rejection when he jumped down from the fence. Fetching a lead rope for Bear, he pulled the horse to a shadier spot alongside the barn. He dared to look into the horse's eyes.

"You know what, Bear? I'm thinking you're probably like me and wouldn't mind feeling a little at home here. Not that I plan to stay or anything, and you might not be here long either. But it would be nice to be on this farm and feel a tiny bit like you're wanted and welcomed. Wouldn't it?"

He started to timidly touch the horse's mane with his fingertips. Just as he did, all at once Bear reared his head then lowered it in the same motion, aiming his nose at Zach's waist. Startled, Zach jumped back. Meanwhile, Bear continued nodding toward Zach's tool-apron as if trying to tell him something. It took a minute for him to realize what Bear wanted. When he did, he laughed out loud.

"*Jah*, you can have this apple for sure. I'm happy to share." He pulled the remaining piece of fruit from the apron pocket. "The apple is from Leah. She cares about you and about my grumpy old *daed* and…"

Suddenly it hit him that Leah was the one person on the farm who didn't seem to have a problem with him. The one person who was concerned enough to put fruit in his pocket. The person who shouldn't be disrespected and who he should be on time to dinner for.

"I'm sorry to cut our visit short, Bear, but I need to get going."

Hurriedly, he got all the horses into the barn and fed them before rushing back to the house. When he arrived, the place was still and silent, and the clock read six forty-five. Leah had left a note that his supper was in the refrigerator. He was thankful for that. Even so, with every bite he couldn't stop thinking of the girl next door. He needed to do something kind for her in return. It wasn't until he'd eaten and got washed up that he figured out what that could be.

Grabbing two bowls and spoons, he placed them in a paper bag. Then he called out to his father to see if he needed anything before leaving. As usual, his father's grunt was his only reply.

While riding into town for the second time that day, he remembered that as a kid, on any summer's night, Dipsy Do's was crowded with customers. It didn't surprise him when it took longer to stand in line and buy ice cream than it did to ride back to Leah's house with it.

As he pulled into her driveway, he was surprised to see her sitting outside, partially covered by the canopy of an oak tree. She looked so cozy, sitting in a cedar chair with her feet tucked under her, that he almost hated to disturb her. Yet as soon as she heard his buggy, she turned and called to him.

"Zach? Is everything all right?"

"*Jah*, I hope so." He exited the buggy and secured his horse to the tree. Then he pulled the bags of treats and bowls from the buggy's back seat. "I wanted to tell you I'm sorry I didn't make it to dinner. I lost track of time. Even so, it was rude of me."

"It's fine. I know you're trying to get a lot done before you leave Sugarcreek."

"*Jah*, I am." More than she knew. He cleared his throat. "But you've been working lots too. I came to thank you for supper. And I, uh…" Suddenly he felt awkward, wondering if she'd seen enough of him for one day. He sure wouldn't blame her, but it was too late to back out. "I thought I'd bring dessert." He held up the bag from the ice cream shop.

"Dipsy Do's? You went all the way into town?"

"Eh, it's a nice night to be out." He reached into the bag, lining up the pints on the wooden table encircled by the four cedar chairs.

She began to laugh softly, and this time he enjoyed hearing her raspy chuckle. "Am I supposed to eat all that by myself?"

"I'm hoping not." He pulled the bowls and spoons from the second bag. "When we were in town today and passed by Dipsy's, you said you hadn't been there in a while. You also mentioned your favorite flavor. I know it started with *p*, but I couldn't remember what it was."

She leaned toward the containers to read them. "So you bought peanut butter chocolate chip, pralines and cream, peppermint, and peach?"

"*Jah.* I wanted to cover all the bases. Which one is your favorite?"

She gave a nervous chuckle. "Oh, you know, I like them all."

Because she was so amiable, she was easier to read than she probably knew. "It's none of these, is it?"

She scrunched her nose, almost apologetically. "I probably mentioned pineapple sherbet, but believe me, all of this will get eaten," she said, quick to put him at ease.

With that, she began spooning heaping mounds of each flavor into her bowl and his too.

"At least, being outdoors, we're not making a mess in your house," he offered.

"And like you said, it's a nice night. Truth is, too, I thought I'd give Thomas and Catherine some alone time. I love my house, but it's a lot smaller than your *daed*'s. It can feel even more cramped when you have a couple that's courting. So it was either sit in my bedroom or—"

"Under the stars."

"*Jah.* A sky full of stars and a bowlful of ice cream. What could be better?"

He nodded in agreement and couldn't remember the last time he'd enjoyed either so much. Even the silence between them while they ate seemed more special than clumsy.

It was a while before Leah spoke up. "Zach, I didn't say it earlier, but I really felt bad that Ivan wasn't more excited about the scooter today."

"It's *oll recht*." He took a bite of peppermint ice cream. "I talked to Bear about it and that helped."

Leah gave him a surprised look, then chuckled. "See what spending time together will do?"

"Oh, *jah*. We're tackling that first step of yours pretty fast."

"Well, you're a likeable guy. I just wish you and your *daed*…" She bit her lip. "I'm sorry. I like you both, and it's hard for me to understand."

Without a doubt, Leah was a person who wanted to make things right. It occurred to him then that maybe he should set things right too. The stars in the sky and the temperature of the air was just like the night of the accident that had caused the wedge between him and his father. Recalling that, and knowing how she felt, made him think the time might be right to explain what had happened.

"Leah…" he started.

Before he could utter another word, Catherine came running out the front door, squealing with all her might. Thomas followed right behind her, trying his best to catch up. Immediately, Zach set down his bowl and Leah did too. They popped up out of their chairs simultaneously.

"Cat, are you okay?" Leah's hand flew to her chest.

"Oh, Leah, *jah*! *Gott* is good, and so is my Thomas. He just proposed to me!" Catherine screeched the news. "We're getting married!"

"Cat, that's *wunderbaar*!"

Leah hugged her cousin wholeheartedly. While the two girls held onto each other jumping up and down, Zach reached out to shake Thomas's hand.

"Congratulations! You two are a *gut* match."

Remembering them as two very likeable *youngies*, Zach meant the words sincerely.

"We're supposed to keep it a secret for just a bit. But I don't know if that's going to happen with Catherine." Thomas grinned.

"Oh, I'm so happy for you both," Leah gushed, breaking away from her cousin to give Thomas a hug. "We need to thank *Gott* and celebrate this union."

"There's plenty of ice cream here." Zach laughed.

"*Jah*, you didn't know your thoughtfulness was going to lead to the perfect celebration." Leah smiled up at him. "I'll run inside and get more bowls."

A half hour later, when their small party broke up due to an outburst of rain, Zach headed the buggy home. Once inside the house, he dutifully and noiselessly opened his father's bedroom door to check on him. He wasn't surprised that his father was sound asleep. But what did astonish him was the sight of the scooter. It had been moved from the far side of the room and was sitting in the corner closest to the bed.

He couldn't stop grinning as he closed his father's door just as quietly as he'd opened it. Walking down the hallway, he felt a hint of hope.

Chapter Five

Since it wasn't a Sunday designated for community worship, the next morning Leah settled into a cushioned chair on her porch with her Bible. After a half hour or so of reading with slightly blurred vision, she paused to praise *Gott* for His Word. She also gave thanks for the sunshine that dappled through the leafy trees and for the sunny people in her life. That included her cousin, of course, and Cat's fiancé who pulled up the drive in his buggy, his horse's glossy dark brown coat gleaming in the light of day.

"*Guder mariye*, Leah." Thomas dipped his straw hat. "Nice weather to be out here feeling close to *Gott*, ain't so?"

"*Jah*, it is," she agreed. "Are you and Cat headed to the woods down the road to do your walking and worshipping?"

"We are as soon as Catherine is ready."

"Congratulations to you again, Thomas. Cat is so excited. She had me up late last night talking about you and the wedding."

"Oh, I hope that wasn't a problem." He frowned. "I know you work hard and need your rest."

She had to smile at his remark. Ever since he and Cat's relationship had grown more serious, Thomas seemed to be trying extra hard to curry favor with her. Which was silly since she already thought of him as a gentle, caring soul who was a good match for her cousin.

"Of course not, Thomas. I'm happy for the both of you."

"You are? For sure?"

"*Verra* much so."

She was surprised at his question and even more taken aback when his shoulders relaxed, and he looked so completely relieved. Hadn't she said the same thing the night before when they celebrated with ice cream? True, sometimes it was hard to be around the two lovebirds. But that wasn't anything that had to do with them. It was only because she grew envious at times, her heart desiring what the happy couple shared. She'd never meant for that to show though. Yet Thomas was a thoughtful sort of man, and she felt badly that he might've sensed moments when jealousy swept over her.

"How about if I go inside and see if Cat is—" She started to stand up when her cousin came rushing out the front door.

"Thomas, my love!" Cat exclaimed exuberantly.

Leah didn't think her cousin's complexion could have been more flushed. That is, until Cat must've realized she'd gushed the words out loud, and Leah noticed her cousin's cheeks turn an even deeper shade of crimson.

However, Thomas didn't appear embarrassed in the least. Rather, he seemed just as overcome with their love, and replied just as affectionately.

"Catherine! My sweet!"

He stepped down from the buggy, having eyes only for his betrothed as he assisted her into the buggy. As they settled next to each other and started to pull away, Cat seemed to remember Leah's existence.

"Leah, I don't know when I'll be back," Cat informed her. "After our worship walk, we're having brunch at the Lehman's. Then we'll be off to tell my parents the news."

"It sounds like a perfect day. Enjoy it," Leah said sincerely.

"We shall!"

Cat's dazzling smile appeared uncontainable, causing Leah to grin too. Even so, once Thomas's buggy took off down the drive and onto the country road, Leah felt her smile diminish, then vanish altogether.

Suddenly, everything around her seemed to go silent. Not even a chirp from a songbird filled her ears. Not one chipmunk or squirrel scurried by. She was unquestionably by herself. Just her alone.

This isn't the first time you've been on your own on a Sunday.

Still, it was the first time since she'd moved to Sugarcreek that she felt so overwhelmingly lonely.

"But I suppose just sitting here and feeling like this isn't helping, is it, Lord?"

She said the words out loud since there was no one nearby to hear except Him. Then she rose to her feet and carried herself and her Bible into the house. Although she wasn't hungry, she needed to do something to curb her anxiousness. She decided on cereal and made a production of cutting banana slices to top the bland-looking flakes before filling the bowl with milk.

Sitting and staring blankly at the cereal box while she barely ate, she sighed. The sound filled the quietude for only a brief second before it was gone too.

Why am I feeling so alone?

Is it because for weeks on end I've been at Ivan's house? Because seven days a week, both night and day, I haven't had a chance to breathe? And now I need to adjust to the change?

But the loneliness clutched at her more intensely than that. And deep down, she knew the real reason why.

Cat was getting married—and soon, all too soon.

Letting go of the spoon, she pushed the bowl away the same way she was trying to push her sad thoughts aside. But it wasn't that easy to do. As she glanced around the place that she called home, tears began to fill her eyes.

When Cat did marry and move away, the house would never feel the same again. There'd be no more late-night talks while sitting in each other's bedrooms, munching on popcorn. No early morning greetings in the kitchen before work. No times on the sofa together, laughing like best friends and sharing like sisters of the heart. Her house would feel bigger. Emptier. Quieter.

Just like it feels at this moment.

She choked back a sob, all the while telling

herself that there was no way she could ever let Cat know what she was feeling. She was genuinely happy for her cousin and would never want to put a damper on her joy. She simply needed to stay positive and find her rhythm again with all the changes to come. And she would, in time, wouldn't she?

Fixated on that thought, she wiped the tears from her cheeks. And welcomed the harsh sound of her chair scooting across the wooden floor as she rose to wash her bowl and spoon. After putting them away, she took a deep breath and wondered what to do next.

Straightening the napkins in the napkin holder took only two seconds.

Folding the dish towel just so on its rod took about three seconds.

And then gazing all around at the emptiness, she suddenly had a thought that brought the slightest smile to her lips. A puppy! Perhaps she needed a canine companion to fill her house and her heart.

Although raising a puppy was a commitment that required a pros and cons list first, didn't it?

She glanced at the shelves above the sink where she typically kept a pad of paper and pens. Instead, her eyes landed on her *gross-mammi*'s recipe box and all thoughts of a furry friend instantly vanished. As she pulled the wooden box down from the shelf and held it tightly against her aching chest, tears flowed once more.

Yet this time the droplets were accompanied by a fond smile and warm memories. Times spent in the kitchen baking with her grandmother had been some of the happiest in her life. She could almost see her *Grossmammi* Sadie clapping gaily like she used to when a pie or cake came out of the oven looking perfect. And there was always that look of gladness on her grandmother's face when she shared her treats at worship or had Leah take them…right next door.

Without a moment's hesitation, Leah set the keepsake box down on the table. It didn't take her long, flipping through the recipes, to find the cherished chocolate chip cake instructions. The paper it was written on was worn and stained with either chocolate or vanilla extract or both. Also, the sheet of paper might've gotten wet at some point because some of her grandmother's handwriting was blurred.

Or was it her eyes doing their funny thing again?

She wasn't sure. All she knew was it felt like *Gott* had given her a sweet gift. And somehow, she would honor His gift.

As she began retrieving ingredients from the cabinets, it did cross her mind that Zach might think it was odd for her to come by on her day off with a cake. But wasn't he the one who'd said that the cake was his favorite? And hadn't he tried so hard just last evening to surprise her with one of her favorites?

She smiled, thinking about his thoughtfulness and all the pints of ice cream he'd delivered to her. Beyond the ice cream, they'd shared an enjoyable time, and she couldn't help but feel a little closer to him.

Yes, just the day before in the grocery her cheeks had flushed when she considered making a cake for Zach. Yet now that she was doing it, the pleasure in creating something special for him was warming her heart too.

Fifteen minutes ago, Zach had been feeling a bit proud of himself. He'd talked his father into spending a part of their Sunday morning together in worship. To do that, he'd even gotten his *daed* to make the trek from the bedroom to the sofa in the living room. But now as Zach sat across from his father reading the Bible out loud to him, he had to stop. Not because he and his father needed to take a minute to let the Scripture sink in. No, it was necessary because Zach's voice was being drowned out by his father's snoring.

The noise was so loud that Zach couldn't even concentrate well enough to read to himself. He got up, thinking he'd search for a quieter spot in the house, when he heard someone knocking at the front door. Seeing Leah standing there, he gladly pushed the screen door wide open.

"Leah, why are you knocking?"

She offered a shy smile. "It seemed the right thing to do since it's my day off."

He chuckled as he glanced at the cake holder in her arms. "And yet it looks like you've been working. Would you like to come in?" he asked softly.

"I don't know. Is this a bad time?" Her eyes questioned him. "You're practically whispering."

He stepped out onto the porch. "It's only because I was reading the Bible to *Daed*, and he—"

"—fell asleep." She finished the sentence for him. "He does that with me a lot too."

"I'm glad to know it's not me. I started wondering if I have a monotone voice." He deliberately raised and lowered his voice with each word, thinking it might capture a smile from

her. It did. "Is that what I think it is?" He nodded to the plastic container in her hands.

"*Jah*, it's the chocolate chip cake that I promised you."

"Now you really have made my day. I appreciate it *verra* much and might even share
some with my father." He winked as he took
the holder from her arms. "And I have sort of
a surprise for you too."

"You do?" She appeared pleased but puzzled.

"Uh-huh." He leaned a little closer and
lowered his voice even more. "When I came
home last night, I checked on *Daed*. And guess
what? He must've used the scooter while I was
gone. It wasn't in the far back corner of the
room anymore."

"Where was it?"

"It was in the corner by the top of his bed."

Her lips instantly curved downward. "Oh,
Zach, I'm sorry to disappoint you. I moved it
there before I left yesterday. So I'm not sure if
that means anything. But it might," she said,
not too convincingly.

"Hmm… I did only call out to him when
I left after dinner last night. I didn't peek in
the room." A slight feeling of disappointment
poked at him momentarily. "It's all right. The
day will come when he's up and flying around

on that thing. Or up and around on his own. In the meantime…"

Suddenly, the perfect weather and the pretty girl standing in front of him tugged at him. It didn't seem right to waste either. "Since it's kind of noisy inside with *Daed*'s snoring, do you want to take a walk or something?"

"I would like that *verra* much." She flashed him a grateful smile which, in turn, made him feel thankful. At least someone was finding pleasure in his suggestions that morning.

Leah waited on the porch while he took the cake inside. As soon as he came back out, he politely asked where she wanted to go.

"Could we go to the creek? I haven't been down there since you cleared out the fallen tree. And that way, if we go there, you won't get to looking around at more work that needs to be done."

He chuckled. "Are you talking about me or you?"

Her hazel green eyes sparkled knowingly. "Probably both of us."

It didn't take much time to get down to the stream. Zach was somewhat surprised when Leah immediately took off her shoes, sat down on the bank, dangled her feet in the water and sighed.

"That nice blue dress of yours may get dirty.

I can run back to the house and get a towel for you to sit on."

"Nee." She shook her head. "My dress will wash fine."

With that, he removed his shoes and sat alongside her. The water was warm from the summer sun but soothing just the same, along with the relaxing sound of it trickling over the rocks and pebbles.

"It's nice that you tried to read to your *daed* earlier, Zach," Leah said after a while.

"One might think so. But truthfully, the more I sat in that chair across from him, I realized I was making the effort more for myself than him." He picked up a dry rock from along the bank, rubbing it between his fingers.

She narrowed her eyes at him. "How so?"

"Ahh…" He drawled out the sound. Somehow, he didn't want her to think less of him. On the other hand, he also wanted to be honest with her. "My *mamm* always sat in that same chair when she'd read to us on Sundays. Of course, back then, I could hardly sit still most of the time," he said, remembering. "But today, I think I wanted to try to recall what those times felt like. *Gott* knows that it was self-serving of me."

He looked over at Leah, somewhat expecting to see judgment in her eyes. Instead, he spied a glimpse of humor.

"And if I'm being honest," she replied, "I didn't make that cake this morning just for you. I made it for me too."

"Does that mean you've already taken some bites out of it?" he teased.

She chuckled. "*Nee*, the cake is intact. But before I baked it, I was feeling so lonely, thinking about Cat moving out in a few months. Then I came across my grandmother's recipe box, and I felt like *Gott* put it in my hands at that moment. It brought back the memories of so many special times that we shared. I was trying to feel that again."

He watched her pluck a strand of tall grass before he spoke. "It's a blessing we have good times in life to reflect on. Even so, maybe they're also reminders that we're still here on earth and need to make some new memories too."

"That's a good way to look at it." She twirled the frond in her hand, looking thoughtful. "I hope you do know that I'm happy for my cousin, because I am."

"Of course, you are. You wouldn't be you if you weren't. Well, that came out a bit awkwardly. But you know what I mean."

She giggled and her eyes shone like the sun. "*Danke*, Zach."

"For what?"

"For making me laugh. I needed that today."

"Leah, I hope you know if you're missing any family you have in West Union, I can take care of *Daed* while you go visit them."

All at once her smile disintegrated. The light left her eyes. "Oh, I...we didn't part on the best of terms."

Her face reddened with embarrassment. Feeling sorry for her, he spoke up. "Now that's something that *I* can relate to." He offered a comforting smile, which seemed to melt her defenses some.

"I guess you can, can't you?"

He nodded. "*Verra* much. But since your parents are gone, is it siblings you're talking about?" He hoped he wasn't prying too much, but he was curious. It was hard to imagine Leah Zook being at odds with anyone.

It was her turn to nod. "I have a sister and two brothers. They're all much older than me. And because of that, since I was the youngest in the family and not yet married, I was left at home to take care of my parents until they went to be with the Lord. Which was fine. But then..."

She paused and bit her lip, making him wonder if she was trying to decide how much to share. Or maybe she simply didn't want to dredge up the past. Again, he could relate.

"It's all right if you don't want to talk about it, Leah."

She shrugged indifferently. Even as she did, her grasp tightened around the stem of grass. "My siblings promised me my parents' home since they had homes of their own, and because I'd also been the one taking care of the house and our parents for years. But shortly after my parents passed, they acted like they'd never said anything of the kind. My sister and brother-in-law moved in with their six *kinner* and pretty much pushed me out. And my brothers took the savings my parents left. Of course, it wasn't losing the house or the money that hurt as badly as how they completely turned their backs on me. It seemed I was only good enough for them while I was helping. As if I wasn't even really family to them."

"That was so cruel of them." His jaw tightened protectively at the injustice. "There was no one to stand up for you?"

"Ha!" she scoffed. "At first I thought my fiancé—ex-fiancé—might."

"You were engaged?"

"Oh, *jah*." She paused and gazed at him quizzically. "Why am I telling you all this?"

"I don't know. Because I confessed first, maybe?"

"I suppose." She sighed before continuing. "Long story short, when my beau learned I was going to inherit the house, he proposed to me. Then, when he found out the house wasn't going to be mine after all, he broke off the engagement. He began courting a *maedel* in town whose family owns a number of shops." She tossed the grass aside and wagged a finger in the air. "Don't ever trust a man whose mind is fixed on money all the time. I learned that lesson too late and won't ever do it again."

He was silent for a moment, wondering what she'd think of a man who didn't exactly *think* of money all the time but had plenty of it. The uncomfortable thought caused him to clear his throat.

"Leah, I'm sorry." He couldn't stop himself from patting her hand, consolingly. "You're such a good person. You didn't deserve what happened to you."

"It's *oll recht*," she said, but he knew she was only trying to put him at ease. "It's over, and I'm fine. It is funny though. I don't often think of my siblings except for when I look over at Stutzman's ice-skating pond on the other side of your *daed*'s property."

"You mean because you skated together in West Union?"

"*Nee*. Again, because of our age difference, we didn't do much together. But we did skate on that pond the one and only time we came to visit *Grossmammi*. It was Christmas and so cold that the shallow water was already frozen."

"Growing up, a lot of us *kinner* skated at Stutzman's."

"Maybe you and I met before and were too young to remember."

"Could be," he agreed. Although it was hard to imagine not remembering someone like Leah. He was working to recall childhood Christmases, when she shyly posed a question.

"Have you, um, ever been engaged?"

"Me?" He blinked. *"Nee."*

"Oh, I just thought maybe—"

"You overheard Uri yesterday in town?" She nodded.

"His sister and I were sweethearts when we were *youngies*, but when I left for Indiana, I didn't ask her to go. It didn't seem right to ask her to leave behind everything she knew and go with me to the unknown. I'm not saying that she would've, but..."

"Still, that was mighty thoughtful of you."

"It was probably the first adult thing I ever did," he admitted.

After that, they sat in comfortable silence, their feet still soaking in the water, until a voice called out to them.

"Finally, I found you!" They both turned to see Matthew striding their way. "I've been looking all over."

Zach stood up, and Leah leaped to her feet right beside him. "Is everything *oll recht, bruder*?"

"It is now. Anna sent me to invite you both to dinner. No way I could head home without tracking you down. I was going to ask *Daed* too, but he's sleeping."

"Not a problem," Zach replied. "We'll bring him along. *Jah?*" He turned to Leah, hoping for a yes.

"Sure. What do you think Anna would like me to bring, Matthew?"

"I don't know." His brother lifted a shoulder. "I guess there's always room for dessert."

Zach looked at Leah, and they both began to chuckle. Matthew eyed them curiously, which only made them laugh even more. As they did, Zach couldn't recall a time in recent years when he'd laughed so hard and experienced such contentment.

For sure, all through his growing up, he'd

enjoyed many happy hours at the creek. But his time spent here with Leah had been even more than that. Sitting on the bank with her, sharing and getting to know her, and then watching her hazel green eyes sparkle with laughter—why, it was more than he'd expected. And he couldn't help feeling, it was unexpectedly good.

Chapter Six

❧

Leah sat at Matthew and Anna's dinner table thinking it was a shame that Ivan said he wasn't in the mood for a ruckus and hadn't come along. True, it was a noisy scene. Samuel and Jonah kept things lively with nonstop fidgeting and chatter. And baby Lydia had chosen suppertime to be fussy.

Even so, if she enjoyed being around the *kinner* and they weren't even related to her, for sure they would've made their grandfather smile too.

"Leah, I hope you know you don't have to mind your manners around this *verrickt* house. If there's anything you want, just help yourself." Matthew pointed to the platters and bowls of food topping the length of the table.

"Danke." She smiled. "I will take another roll." She reached over for the breadbasket.

Then she said, "Anna, everything is so delicious. But I can't imagine how you had a minute to fix all this food. Next time, you all need to come to my house, and I'll do the cooking."

Leah hadn't been around Matthew and Anna's family much since she'd moved to Sugarcreek, but when she had, she'd always felt comfortable around them. They were both genuinely kind and easy to talk to.

"That would be a real treat, Leah. Count us in any time you're in the mood for an evening of chaos." Anna grinned. "Speaking of your house, I have been wondering when my cousin will be moving out. I think she and Thomas will be announcing their wedding plans soon, don't you think?"

Leah knew she shouldn't be the one to tell Cat's news. As it was, her cousin had been overly excited and had revealed Thomas's proposal before going through the proper channels.

Zach didn't disclose anything either. Instead, he looked up at Anna and chuckled. "You've always got marriage on your mind, don't you?"

"Why, *jah*. I want everyone to join our club." Anna winked at him, and Leah figured there was a kind of joke between Zach and his sister-in-law by the way they looked at each other.

"Our club is a happy place to be," Matthew

said before turning to his youngest son. "Jonah, the mashed potatoes are for eating. They're not for building a tower with your hands."

"I'm sure Catherine and Thomas will find it happy too," Anna agreed, "when the time comes."

Leah nodded. "They'll be perfect together."

Zach glanced over at her. "If Catherine is a cousin to both of you, are you and Anna related somehow?"

"*Nee*. It's funny how it turns out." Leah chuckled. "Catherine and Anna are second cousins because of their mothers being first cousins. Cat and I are first cousins because our fathers were brothers."

"That's unbelievable." Zach shook his head.

"*Jah*, small world," Anna agreed while swaying side to side, trying to soothe Lydia. "Samuel, sit down in your seat all the way, please. And, Jonah, eat five more peas. Can you count them for him, Samuel?"

"Why can't he do it?" Samuel whined. "I counted when I was three."

"Well, I sure couldn't," Matthew chimed in. "When I was your age, Samuel, and your *Onkel* Zach was three, he taught me a thing or two. He was always better at numbers and fixing things than me."

"And you were always better at organizing

projects and people than I was." Leah noted Zach's grin before he continued. "Sometimes you even had the Stutzman boys doing your chores for you, Matthew. And me, too, now that I'm thinking about it."

Everyone laughed, but Leah noticed that most of what was said had gone over Samuel's head. The boy still looked annoyed.

"Want me to help you teach your *bruder* to count, Samuel?"

The five-year-old nodded eagerly, and Leah got up and stood between the boys' two chairs. She instructed Samuel to move one pea at a time and say the number, then have Jonah say the number until there were five peas set aside on Jonah's plate. Not only did Samuel appear pleased to have the upper hand and to be giving directions to his little brother, but Jonah must've thought those peas were extra special at that point. All at once, he cupped the five of them in his small hand and slurped them up in one bite.

"Leah, now I know why I heard some *mamms* saying what a whiz you are, tutoring reading to their children," Anna said as Leah sat back down in her seat. "You're a natural-born teacher."

"Oh, I..." Leah shook her head, feeling her

cheeks flush uncontrollably at the compliment. *"Danke."*

"You said you liked to read," Zach spoke up. "But I didn't know you tutored reading."

"Well, aren't you glad you're back in Sugar-creek so you can learn a few things?" Anna raised a playful brow at Zach while Matthew chuckled at his *frau*'s comment. "Before your *daed*'s accident, Leah had been tutoring students in a corner of Sunshine Bakery. And mothers were thankful that she did," Anna said, continuing her praise.

Zach shot Leah an astonished look. "That's amazing."

"It's reading, Zach." She smiled. "Not physics or engineering."

"And she did it for free," Anna added. "She volunteered her time."

"Volunteered?" Matthew frowned. "Sounds like you need a business manager."

"What she probably needs—" Anna spoke over the rising commotion of the *kinner* "—is some peace and quiet around the dinner table."

Leah laughed as she saw the boys tapping each other's shoulders with their spoons while the baby girl fussed in Anna's arms.

"I've been enjoying this just fine. The company. The food. Everything. *Danke* for having me. I'm wondering though—may I take little

Lydia off your hands, Anna, so you can enjoy the *wunderbaar* meal you cooked too?"

"I wouldn't mind if you did."

Anna passed baby Lydia over to her, and the chatter continued among the adults and boys until everyone finished eating. With full stomachs all around, everyone agreed they'd wait a bit for dessert. After helping to clear the table, the men took the boys outside to run off some energy. Leah was more than happy to start on the dishes while Anna took Lydia upstairs to change her into nightclothes.

When Anna returned to the kitchen, she placed Lydia in a bouncy seat next to the table. Hearing the baby girl springing up and down, cooing and gurgling to her heart's content, Leah was surprised. Lydia didn't even seem like the same child.

"She looks so happy right now," Leah said as she rinsed the last of the plates and placed it in the drying rack.

Anna laughed. "*Jah*, during supper she always refuses the bouncy seat. I think she likes being held and seeing all that's going on. But quite often when I'm at the sink doing the dishes like you just were, she's right at home with it."

"Is that so, *boppli* girl?" Leah stepped over and held out her index finger to the little one.

Lydia grabbed it, bouncing even more, causing Leah to feel a pure sense of joy well up inside her.

"I'm feeling pretty much at home myself right now," she whispered to the child.

After all, she couldn't believe how just that morning, she'd been feeling miserable. Then *Gott* had brightened her day in a way she would've never imagined. She was just about to tell Anna thank you once again when Zach's sister-in-law exclaimed her name.

"Oh, Leah!"

"Jah?" Leah turned from Lydia to see Anna standing over the open cake holder on the table. "What is it?"

"Is this a chocolate chip cake? The same one your *grossmammi* Sadie used to make? The cake Matthew has been begging me to bake ever since we've been married?"

Leah chuckled at Anna's description. "It is," she confirmed. "It's a favorite of Zach's, too, it seems. I suppose the Graber men will have to fight over it."

"Jah, and I'm sure the young *buwes* will take after them." Anna grinned. "Hopefully, we'll get a piece for ourselves."

"Maybe we should cut our slices before I call them inside."

"*Gut* thinking, my wise friend." Anna snickered. "Let me grab some plates."

It wasn't too long after enjoying Leah's delicious cake that the evening came to an end. Zach helped Leah into his buggy and before starting for home, they both turned toward the porch to wave their goodbyes. They waved to Anna and Matthew, who had his arm around his wife's waist. To his nephews, who were hugging their father's legs. And to little Lydia, who was peacefully slumbering on her mother's shoulder.

Seeing Matthew's family that way brought on something that Zach had never experienced before. Because for the first time he truly saw where his brother lived. Not simply in a dwelling with a roof over his head. But in a home. A real home with a beloved family tucked inside.

As Zach mindlessly steered Sugar onto the open road, he realized that Matthew might've only been two years older than him, but he was eons ahead of Zach in terms of finding his place in the world and a true foundation. He was thinking about that when Leah spoke up, bringing him out of his reverie.

"I had a *verra* nice time, Zach. Thank you for having me come along."

"It was a good way to spend a Sunday evening, wasn't it? And you don't have to thank me, Leah. Matthew and Anna wanted you to come," he reminded her. "And I'm glad you did too. It wouldn't have been the same without you." He was surprised he said as much. But it was true, wasn't it?

"You mean because there wouldn't have been the chocolate chip cake for you and Matthew to vie for?"

"Well, there was that." He glanced at her and grinned. "But everyone got along so well. You and Anna have a lot in common, I think." Getting to know Leah more in the past weeks, the thought had crossed his mind several times. The two women were not only kindhearted and giving—they were smart, loyal and enjoyable to be around. Not to mention easy on the eyes.

Of course, he wasn't about to say all of that out loud—or any of it, actually.

"Oh, I don't know about that." She shook her head. "I'm not sure I could be as patient as Anna is, being around three *kinner* all day."

"You say that, but you take care of my father, and I'd say he equals out to at least two *kinner*." He chuckled, then caught himself. Maybe Leah wouldn't appreciate a remark like that, even though he meant it lovingly. "I'm sorry. That probably wasn't kind of me to say."

"But it is true. And the truth isn't always so

kind." She grinned. "Why, when I got those chances to tutor, I had a couple of five-year-old boys who behaved better than your *daed* does sometimes."

They both laughed. It was evident that they each loved his father in their own way. As he steered the buggy down the empty road past fields filled with chirping crickets, he couldn't stop thinking how much Leah had sacrificed for his father.

"You really need to get back to tutoring again, Leah," he blurted. "You need to do something for yourself. I'm sure you miss it."

"I do, and I long to. But it doesn't feel right to be starting it up again. I promised your *daed* that we'd both get back to doing the things we love—training horses and tutoring. And that hasn't happened for him yet. So why should I be able to and he can't? That doesn't seem right."

He glanced at her, thinking her heart was too big for her own good. "But I'm here now, Leah. And while I am here, you should take advantage of that."

She stole a glance at him before settling her eyes on her hands in her lap. It was a minute before she replied.

"Do you have any idea how long you'll be staying, Zach? I mean, just so I could tell parents how long I'd be tutoring," she added in a rush. "That is, if I decide to start up again."

"I'll stay as long as I need to," he found himself promising. "Until the time is right, and things get more settled."

Funny, when he first arrived in Sugarcreek, he'd been counting the days till he could leave. And now…

Glancing over at Leah, he wondered why he hadn't been thinking that way as much lately. Of course, he wasn't yet close to establishing a secure future for his father and setting things right with him. So there was that. But he also kept finding out things about the woman sitting next to him that for some reason piqued his curiosity each day.

"Did you ever want to become a teacher?" he blurted out of nowhere.

"Me?" She arched a brow, obviously as surprised by his question as he was. "Oh, *nee*. But I…" She paused and fidgeted with her hands, appearing anxious about sharing.

"But you what?" He couldn't help himself from nudging. He offered what he hoped was a warm smile.

"Well, besides tutoring reading, I dream of having a space in town that's a reading room for children, or for anyone actually. It'd be a cozy spot with lots of bookshelves and cushy chairs where people can come and relax and read or meet friends and talk about books or whatever. There could be treats from the bakery and cold sandwiches from Kauffman's Kitchen and…" She seemed to sense she was getting carried away and caught herself. "But that's, uh…the only thing I've done so far is tutor a few Amish and *Englisch* children here and there, like Anna mentioned."

"Still, Leah, that doesn't sound like an impossible dream. You should be working toward that for sure." He hoped he sounded encouraging while inwardly he felt somewhat frustrated. If she only knew the truth about him and his financial resources—that he could make that happen for her in an instant.

"I will, all in good time." She sighed, then flickered her long lashes almost apologetically. "Zach, I feel like you've gotten me blabbing about myself a lot today. You seem to have that effect on me and Bear lately."

His lips curved upward. "Bear's vocabulary isn't as evolved as yours. But you're right. I have been getting to know him a little better. Though we're not quite best friends yet."

"I'm sure you two will get there." She giggled before asking, "And what about you? Do you have a dream? When I came out to tell you and Matthew that dessert was being served, I overheard you two talking. You were saying something about contacting a property development company next week. Is that something you're getting into doing?"

All at once, his hands tightened around the buggy reins. A flash of heat surged up the back of his neck and his mouth instantly went dry. His mind raced, trying to land on something to say.

How could he answer her without lying?

How long could he keep holding back information from her? Especially when he knew the wish of her heart. She wanted his father to get back to doing what he loved—training horses. Every time she mentioned that, he felt his stomach clench with guilt, knowing that wasn't what he had in mind at all. But Matthew had already warned him to be cautious about sharing their intentions until things were more in place. Realistically, that wasn't such a bad idea, was it?

Finally, he answered her, feigning an offhandedness he didn't feel. "We weren't talking about me exactly. The property development company is something I'm looking into for someone else."

"Oh, I thought I heard you say that you—"

He interrupted, guessing what she'd heard. Both he and Matthew had jumped when she'd come out to the porch to get them. They'd glanced at each other, and he knew his brother was wondering how long she'd been standing behind them.

"Someone I know owns some property here in Sugarcreek, and I'm going to get a feel for the Highland Property Development Company since I've sort of been associated with that kind of business before." He tried to explain briefly and as close to the truth as he could. "I'm going to set up the meeting as if I'm the one selling."

"Sounds complicated. That sort of business isn't something I have a mind for." She waved a hand. "But I'm sure the person who owns the property is glad that you're wired that way."

He hated that he couldn't tell her everything. But looking over at her and seeing she was gazing out into the night with a smile on her face, he thought maybe it was best that he didn't. Why ruin what had been a perfect evening? Besides, she turned to him abruptly, and it seemed her mind had already shifted elsewhere.

"I wish your *daed* had come out tonight. He really would've enjoyed himself." She sat up straighter. "And I was thinking. Remember earlier today when you asked if I'd moved the scooter? I said I had, but I didn't say where exactly."

"*Jah*, you did." He gave her a curious frown. "You said you moved it to the top of his bed."

"And I did. I took it from the rear right corner of the room to the top right corner near his bed. Where did you see it again?"

"On the left side closest to the door."

"The left side? Really?"

"Really and truly."

"Oh, Zach! He used the scooter!" Something about her hoarse, raspy voice in the biggest squeal ever made him laugh mirthfully. Well, that and the joy of knowing his father had gotten up to give the scooter a try. "You did it! You got him moving!" she exclaimed.

"*Nee, we* did it, or we're doing it, I guess. I mean *Daed*'s doing it."

He was so crazily happy that he wasn't sure what he was saying. Overjoyed, he loosened his grip on the reins and reached for Leah's hand with his free one. Then raising their clasped hands, he said, "*Danke, Gott.* Thank You."

"Amen, amen," Leah shouted happily. "Being the proud man that Ivan is, I'm sure he'll be scooting around in front of everyone when he masters it more."

"I know you're right," Zach agreed and squeezed her hand and held on tight. As soon as he realized what he'd done in his excitement, he released his grasp instantly. "I'm sorry. I got carried away."

"I understand."

And he knew she did. Because even a few minutes later down the road, when he glanced over at her, the exuberant smile had yet to disappear from her face. Seeing that, he felt his joy rekindled all over again. For sure, it felt good to have someone to share his father's small triumph with.

Still, as he steered the buggy into Leah's drive, his conscience niggled at him unmercifully. The day couldn't come too soon when he could finally be totally truthful with her.

Chapter Seven

Nearly two weeks later, Leah stepped into Sunshine Bakery and a rush of excitement tickled her stomach. Looking around the shop, a feeling of gratitude came over her as well. She'd come early to get ready for her tutoring sessions with the young Amish and *Englisch* children who'd been signed up. But at a glance, she could see Cat and Marianne had beaten her to that.

"You've already set up the table and chairs in the corner for me," she said, turning to the two of them standing behind the counter. "*Danke.* You are too good to me."

"Not a problem," Cat replied as she took her time precisely arranging iced cupcakes on a tiered stand. "We wanted everything to be just right for your first time back to tutoring. Also, to celebrate your grand re-opening," her cousin added, smiling, "Marianne and I decided that we'll be giving away a cupcake to each of your students when they leave today." Cat set the filled cupcake stand on the countertop, then brushed her hands over her apron.

Leah was so overwhelmed by their thoughtfulness, her cheeks warmed. Even to her own ears, her voice sounded more hoarse than usual. "You ladies are so sweet. I can't believe all you've thought to do." She glanced at her cousin and then at Marianne, an *Englischer* around their same age who had been working at the bakery since she was a teenager.

"And there's one more thing," Marianne said. "Did you see the new addition? I brought a chair I found stored in my grandmother's basement." She pointed to a cozy-looking, blue-cushioned armchair not too far from where Leah typically read with the children. "The moms can sit there and rest comfortably while you're working with their child."

"I… I don't know what to say," Leah stammered. "You both have gone out of your way to make the perfect setting."

The ladies looked at each other and smiled. "It's simple," Marianne replied. "You can promise to tutor my children when they come along." She patted her stomach.

"Marianne, are you—"

"I'm due in six months." The married woman's eyes lit up.

"Congratulations! And now I'm really thinking you shouldn't have been lifting that chair."

"Oh, I didn't. My husband Jason helped with that."

"And after I'm married, I'll be right behind Marianne." Cat linked an arm with her co-worker friend. "Our children will be keeping you busy for years to come, Leah. But for now, I'm just glad that Zach talked you into tutoring again. Not only because you love it, but it's a fun diversion for us as well."

"Zach wasn't going to stop hounding me about it, that's for sure."

"It's always nice when a man isn't afraid to push a woman toward her dreams," Marianne chimed in.

"*Jah*, he's been pushy for sure."

Leah laughed, but deep down she'd been touched by Zach's prodding. Not only had he started urging her to get back to tutoring the evening they'd been at Matthew and Anna's for dinner, but he'd kept encouraging her ever since.

He was the one who insisted she shouldn't feel bad doing something she enjoyed since Ivan was healing some too. Zach's father was coming to the table for more of his meals now, sometimes propping his leg up on an extra chair. And when Zach had taken Ivan to his most recent doctor's appointment, the results of the imaging tests thankfully revealed that Ivan was healing fine. He was just a few weeks away from turning in his cast for a walking boot.

Already thinking that would be the case, Zach had contacted Cat. The two of them had gone behind Leah's back, posting a sign-up sheet for her tutoring sessions on the bakery's bulletin board. In the end, Leah was glad the two of them had been so secretive. Otherwise, she would've been holding her breath while wondering if she'd have any takers.

Fortunately, all the afternoon spots filled up, and Cat burst into the house after work at the start of the week, happy to present Leah with the list. However, that didn't leave much time for her to go to the library and check out age-appropriate books. She also went through her things at home, packing her tote with games and puzzles that she'd used before. Her prior tutoring experience might've been brief. But she'd quickly learned that a change of activity could be helpful when a young child got antsy in their seat.

As she began emptying the contents of her bag onto the table, she couldn't stop from musing about the truth of what Marianne had said about Zach. In the past weeks, he had supported her and cheered her on more than any man in her life ever had. Even before she'd left the farm to come to town, he'd made sure to wish her well and let her know he'd take good care of Ivan while she was gone. She smiled inwardly. As if she didn't trust that he would.

She was just trying to think of how she could thank him, short of baking another chocolate chip cake, when Cat called out to her.

"Miss Leah, your first student has arrived."

She'd been so caught up in her thoughts and organizing her reading materials that she hadn't heard the shop's door chime. Her stomach quivered nervously as she headed toward the door, until she saw Pamela Clarkson and her daughter Charlotte standing there. In an instant the feeling dissipated, and she couldn't hide the smile bursting across her face. Nor did she want to.

"Hello! I've missed you," she greeted them.

"Charlotte has missed you, too, Miss Leah," Pamela replied, stroking her daughter's blond curls. "We were both so glad to see your sign-up sheet posted again."

Charlotte nodded shyly. "I brought a book from home."

"You did? Can I see?"

Charlotte glanced at her mother, who pulled the book from her purse. "You don't have to read this if it messes with your reading plans." Pamela handed the copy to Leah.

"Shelley Shell?" Leah read the title out loud. "I can't believe you brought this, Charlotte. Of course, we can read it. And guess what book I got you?"

"What?" Charlotte's eyes grew wide.

"Knowing how much you like the ocean, I found *Fishy Fish* at the library."

With that, Charlotte giggled and grabbed Leah's hand, causing Pamela to laugh.

"Um, I think she's totally comfortable. I'm going to get situated in that chair over there." She pointed to the blue seat. "It's new, isn't it?"

Leah nodded. "And fit for moms."

Leah felt blessed to get off to a grand start with Charlotte as her initial student. The other young boys and girls that followed were delightful to spend time with as well. Even so, at the end of all the sessions, as Leah was packing up books and games, she felt somewhat dismayed. While the children had been more than cooperative, her eyes hadn't. There were times she'd found herself struggling over the printed words as much as her students. Beyond that, every so often shimmering spots of light showed up at the outside corners of her vision.

"That's a big sigh," Cat said, coming up alongside her.

"Did I sigh?" She turned to look at her cousin and cringed.

"Uh, *jah*, kind of loudly. Sounds like you may need a cupcake. I put some in there for Ivan and Zach too." She handed Leah a plastic container. "Was it a rough afternoon? From what I saw, it looked like you and the *kinner* were enjoying yourselves."

"I was. We were. The sessions all went so well, and everyone signed up for next time. It's just... I don't know." She squinted. "My eyes had a mind of their own this afternoon. They weren't being too cooperative. But now they seem better again. It's strange."

"I'm sure glasses could help."

"Maybe," Leah replied uncertainly.

"Oh, my. You're not set against wearing glasses because you have a thing for Zach, are you? I'm sure you'd be beautiful to him either way."

"Catherine, please." Leah shook her head. "I don't know why you keep bringing Zach up to me. We're working together to try to help Ivan. That's all, and you know it."

Cat quirked a smile. "I've watched when you're together. You both laugh a lot."

Leah lifted a brow. "Isn't that what people do when something's funny?"

She wasn't sure if it was the silly conversation or the past hours of working to focus her eyes that was causing her head to throb. Rubbing her forehead, she sighed again. "I'm sorry if I'm being testy. I loved tutoring the children today, but that sun coming in the window kept hitting the sides of my eyes. And then, too, my eyes got blurry while reading."

"The sun?" Cat's forehead creased. "Leah, it's been overcast most of the afternoon."

"Oh." She glanced out the window and saw that her cousin was right. "Well, I don't know what it was then. But it was something."

"Cousin, you really need to go to the drugstore and get some reading glasses. Or better yet, make an eye doctor's appointment. You're probably farsighted and maybe even have some astigmatism. I know a good number of my customers do."

Leah crinkled her nose. "How would you know? It's nothing you can see on a person, can you?"

"Of course, you can't. But trust me, people share with me plenty on this job. More than I want to hear at times." Cat rolled her eyes.

"You do bring home a lot of stories." Leah laughed, placing the strap of her full tote bag over her shoulder. "I'm going to take your advice. I don't know why I've been putting off seeing someone. Especially when there's probably a simple solution to this eye thing I've been having."

"*Jah.* It's not like you have some hereditary eye disease and are going blind like *Aenti* Naomi Zook."

"*Aenti* who?"

Cat waved a hand, dismissing her question. "Just go take care of yourself, okay? So then you can take care of your students."

How could Leah argue with that?

After thanking Cat and Marianne once more, she took a determined left out of the bakery door. The eye doctor's office was a quick two-block walk up the street. She walked in, thinking the most she could do would be to make a future appointment. But at least it would be a good place to start.

However, the woman at the front desk informed her differently. "We just had a cancellation. If you have time, Dr. Hobbs can see you right now."

All afternoon, admittedly, she'd been questioning *Gott.* Wondering why He'd given her the opportunity to tutor again when her eyes didn't quite seem up to the task. Yet by the time she followed an assistant back to an exam room and was seated there, it was amazing how quickly her attitude had changed.

Forgive me, Lord, for my questioning You. Danke *for putting up with me like You always do!*

Her prayer was sincere, and her heart was, too, as the doctor entered into the room.

Zach crossed his arms over his chest and gave his father a long, hard stare.

"*Daed*, all day you've been sitting in this living room."

"So what?"

His father's sharp tone often caused Zach to instinctively grind his teeth, which was exactly what was happening in that moment. "So, you can back out on me all you want. But you promised Leah that you'd get outside today."

"I'm sure it's mighty hot out there."

"If you stepped out the door, you'd see it's a little cloudier than it has been." Zach knew that for a fact. He'd been working outdoors all day, except when he had to keep coming inside to nudge his father. "*Daed*, Leah is going to be getting home from town soon. And when she finds out that you lied to her, she—"

"I didn't lie." His father scowled. "I changed my mind."

Zach took off his hat, ran his fingers through his hair and worked to regain his patience.

"Look, *Daed*, I'm going to go out and finish up one of the things on my list and then—"

His father interrupted once more. "What list?"

Zach's jaw clenched. "It's not a big deal. Just some things to tidy up." And repair. And paint. And… "Either you come outside now, or I'm coming back in ten minutes and getting you. You're not breaking your promise to that sweet girl."

"Oh, *oll recht*." His father groaned. "You can stop your fussing. I'll come now."

It wasn't as if Zach was insensitive to his father. But he knew it wasn't helpful, physically or mentally, if his *daed* rarely got up and tried to move around. Although Zach had to smile inwardly. His father wasn't hurting when it came to his usual way of being difficult.

"You said you'd help me with the horses," Zach said, helping his father to his feet.

"You're making things up. I can't get around that good yet."

"Oh, I probably heard you say that when you were talking in your sleep." He tried a teasing tone. However, no smile erupted on his father's face. Only the opposite—a frown.

"I don't talk in my sleep."

Though his father seemed annoyed as usual, Zach was glad that he allowed him to help while they slowly descended the porch steps. Ever cautious, Zach supported him with a strong, tight hug underneath his shoulders the entire way. Once they got to the bottom, he led his *daed* over to the scooter that he'd previously moved there. His *daed* looked a bit unsteady as he started to board the scooter. But when Zach reached out to lend a hand, this time his father pushed him away.

"Where do you think we're going?" his father asked once he got settled on the device.

Zach nodded toward the barn. "I assumed you'd want to see your horses and the newer one too. I've been calling him Bear for now because of his personality." A not-so-kind but honest thought flashed through his mind that it could also be a nickname for his father. "He isn't trained by any means, but he's getting more comfortable in his surroundings. Leah gave me a three-step process to help build his trust."

"She did, huh?" His father's lips tightened. "It's a long way over to the barn. And my ribs are still hurting."

"I hear ribs can be *verra* painful and slow healing. Let me get the golf cart."

His father instantly cuffed a hand over Zach's wrist. "*Nee.* Who told you to get that thing and this scooter anyway?" his father barked. "It all costs money."

"*Daed*, they're both rentals. It's not yours to worry about."

Despite his father's prior protest, they ventured on at a slow pace. Once they reached the fence surrounding the pasture, his father started to disembark the scooter. Permitting just the slightest assistance from Zach, he latched onto the top rail with his hands. Pulling himself up, he stood on his good foot, letting his casted ankle dangle in the air. He exhaled loudly, and Zach knew it had been a workout for him.

They stood eyeing the horses grazing in the pasture, not sharing a word. Until his father muttered something.

"I'm sorry. What did you say?" Zach asked.

"Nothing." His father turned to go.

"*Daed*, we just got here."

"I've been here long enough."

As they made their way back to the house in silence, not even grousing at each other for a change, Zach felt somewhat bad that he'd urged his father to visit the horses in the first place. He thought it'd put his *daed* in a better frame of mind, but it hadn't seemed to at all.

And what was the point of it anyway? Zach reprimanded himself. In a way, it was almost cruel of him to put his father in that situation when, in turn, he was doing all he could to remove the responsibility of those horses from his father's life.

Zach shook his head at himself, befuddled by his own actions. Had he made the suggestion on his own behalf? Maybe so that his father would see he'd been taking good care of the creatures? Something that his father never thought he had the mind or heart to do?

Thankfully, the comforting sound of Leah's familiar voice pulled him from his sour thoughts. She practically glowed as she stood on the porch awaiting them.

"Hello, you two. Guess what? Cat sent me home with cupcakes for both of you."

His father spoke up right away. "*Gut*, I'm hungry."

Zach looked directly at Leah and held up his hands. "Don't blame me. I fed *Daed* lunch right after you left just like you told me to."

She chuckled. "I suppose being outdoors can give a man an appetite."

Zach left it unsaid that they hadn't been outside for long at all.

"Why don't you have a seat on the porch?" she suggested to his father. "And I'll get you a glass of iced tea and a cupcake. Chocolate, right?"

"*Jah, danke.*"

It was the first time Zach had seen his father smile even the slightest all day. After helping his father up the steps and into a chair, he followed Leah into the house and told her so.

"I'm thankful you have that effect on him." He left it unsaid that she had the same effect on him plenty of times too.

"Oh, *jah*. Once in a great while, I do."

"How were your tutoring sessions, by the way?"

"Wunderbaar," she said breathlessly. "I can't thank you enough, Zach, for pushing me to do it again. Without you…" Her hazel green eyes shone as she looked up at him, drawing him in completely. Leaving him hoping there would come a day when he could help her even more. "I mean, without your coaxing me and being here for your *daed*," she continued, "I don't know that I would have tried again."

"I only did what you do for others, Leah. You encourage them." He gave her an earnest look but seeing how her cheeks flushed, he changed the subject instantly. "How were your students?"

"Well, Charlotte was first. I think I mentioned that I'd had her before and—"

"What's taking so long?" His father's voice came loud and clear through the screen door.

"We're coming, Mr. Graber," Leah answered

kindly before turning to Zach. "Do you mind getting the tea, and I'll get the cupcake?" There she was again. Immediately placing someone else's needs above her own.

"I will. As long as you promise to tell me later about the good stuff that happened at your sessions."

She looked at him and seemed to pause for a moment. "*Jah*, I will. Promise."

As he grabbed a glass from the cupboard, he quipped, "Wouldn't it be nice if *Daed* asked for things just a little more politely once in a while? Sometimes his brusqueness tends to embarrass me."

"I don't know. You'd probably have a heart attack if he ever said please." She laughed. "I guess I'm used to it by now. And sometimes I think he gets tired of seeing the same faces."

"Maybe mine. But yours isn't so bad." He winked.

"Not so bad, huh?" She bit her lip as she placed a chocolate cupcake on a plate. "Hmm. I suppose I'll take that as a compliment." She giggled. "As for your *daed*, I think it'll be a nice change for him when everyone comes for his birthday dinner on Saturday."

"Your positive attitude is appreciated, Miss Leah. That's what your students call you, right?"

He handed her the glass filled with iced tea, then held the screen door open as she went to serve his father. As he watched the two of them, he wondered if despite Leah's optimism, she saw the same thing in his father that he did.

Because for as long as he'd known his *daed*, his father's gray-blue eyes had always appeared determined and intent. Whereas these days, even with a kind woman doting on him, his stare looked distant and hollow. And whether they shared much of a closeness anymore, that was something that disturbed Zach immensely. For him, seeing another man look that way— any man—was unsettling.

And while Zach didn't doubt that his father's land had value, could it be that his *daed* was feeling that he didn't? Was that why he'd been so slow to get out of bed? Was he feeling lost, not sure what he could look forward to?

Zach wished they had the kind of relationship that they could talk things through. But since they didn't, he'd simply have to keep moving forward with his and Matthew's plan. What else could he do?

Chapter Eight

Leah dipped her brush into the can of white paint sitting on a tarp atop Ivan's porch. As she did it, she glanced over at Zach and sighed wistfully. Most *maedels* she knew would be sighing over his broad shoulders and strong-looking, capable hands. And, no doubt, those were things she never failed to notice and admire about him.

Yet this Saturday morning, she also found herself just as awestruck by his painting technique. His motion as he painted over a window shutter was utterly fluid. Meanwhile, it had been taking her several good blinks of her blurry eyes every time she dared to run her brush over the wooden handrail.

Zach must've sensed her staring. He stopped painting and turned to look at her. "Everything *oll recht*?" he asked.

"*Jah, jah.* I was just thinking you're mighty good at this painting business."

He cocked his head and grinned. "There's no reason I wouldn't be. I've done plenty of it for many years while making a living."

"Then I shouldn't feel so bad. I've only painted a mailbox once." She crinkled her nose. "And it dried with lots of drippy streaks."

His blue eyes twinkled instantly. "You know what, Leah?"

"That I should maybe practice before taking on a job? Is that what you were going to say?"

"That's not what I was thinking at all. I was, uh…" His voice softened as his expression grew more serious. "I was thinking that you always have a way of making me smile."

She was so taken aback by his comment, and even more by the sincere look in his eyes, that at first, she wasn't sure how to respond. However, her cheeks seemed to know how to react. Unfortunately, she could feel her face flush pink immediately.

"What I mean is, you don't care what people think. You're open and honest. And it's good you're that way. Not many people are."

She dipped her head some, hoping he wouldn't spy her blushing. "*Danke,* Zach. And right now," she said, changing the subject abruptly for her own sake, "I'm honestly hoping I can get better at painting *verra* quickly."

"Everything in its time." He smiled. "And not to be bossy, but it looks like you missed a section at the bottom of the rail post there." He pointed to the spot.

"Okay, *danke*."

As she made her way back over to the railing, she could somewhat see the area he was speaking of. But her vision wasn't as clear as she would've liked. They'd opted for the mid-morning sunlight since it wasn't too bright nor the temperature too hot for painting. Yet she kept sensing the same shimmers of light at the outside corners of her eyes like she'd experienced during her tutoring lesson. Which led to plenty of squinting.

The idea of having to order prescription eyeglasses had taken some getting used to. But each day that her eyes continued acting up, more and more she was looking forward to having glasses as soon as they were ready.

Silly as it was, she was lost in thought, imagining everyone's reaction to seeing her in eyeglasses when her paintbrush finally went dry again. Apparently the same was true of Zach's brush. They met up at the paint can at the exact same time.

"I've been having trouble with my eyes, and I'm getting glasses," she blurted.

"You are, huh? Are you farsighted or near-sighted?"

"Farsighted and with astigmatism."

His brows rose. "Ah."

"Ah, what?"

"And here I thought you were perfect." He shook his head, pretending to be disappointed.

She slugged his shoulder playfully in response.

"Since you're sharing, I'll have you know that I happen to have a lazy eye." He turned his head slightly, pointing to his left eye. "It's a very mild case. I did some therapy for it when I was younger."

"And here I thought you were perfect as well."

"Pretty close. But you've probably noticed that I squint sometimes."

"*Jah*, I have. I just thought you were eyeing me skeptically."

"And that does happen a lot." He chuckled. "Especially on days like this. I still can't believe you have us painting this morning when we have plenty to do to get ready for *Daed*'s birthday dinner later on."

She raised her hand, defensively. "But you didn't try to talk me out of it."

"Do you really think I could've?"

"I don't know. You can be persuasive at times."

"Name one time."

"Like when you said you'd make the barbecue ribs and chicken for tonight's dinner while I make the cheesy potato casserole, beans and birthday cake."

"I didn't say that. You came up with that plan."

"Oh, you're right." She cocked her head. "Well, that's because we make such a good team in the kitchen."

"I can't argue with that."

She wondered if he said that while remembering the last time they'd cooked together. A smile crossed her lips simply thinking about it. They'd started out with their own ideas about what made up the perfect spaghetti sauce. But then they'd stood shoulder to shoulder over the simmering pot while adding each of their special ingredients. As it turned out, the sauce was the best she'd ever tasted.

"At least we don't have to decorate. Anna is bringing balloons, which the boys will like too."

"If the balloons make it here in one piece," he quipped. "Leah, are you sure you don't mind Samuel staying for the week?"

She knew Anna was planning to take baby Lydia and head to Murray, Kentucky. Her sister there had recently given birth to a set of twins and needed Anna's help. Jonah was staying in town with a family who had a son his age. Leah was happy to think that Samuel had a welcome place to stay as well. Which meant Matthew wouldn't have to worry about any of his *kinner* while he was at work for the week.

"Why would I mind, Zach? It'll be a fun change." The mere thought of it truly warmed her heart. "Plus, I think it will be nice for your *daed* to be around his grandson. In all the time that I've lived next door, I haven't seen him interact with his grandchildren very much."

"I'm sure Samuel will want us to do things with him constantly. You know how busy young *buwes* are. It's doubtful we'll get much work accomplished this week."

Leah knew he was referring to the items on the maintenance list and started to ask what all was left to do. But in truth, she didn't want to know. After Zach's recent work on the farm, she could tell the property was more groomed than she'd ever seen it. Realizing all the work would be completed in the near future, she felt her stomach tighten. That meant Zach would be leaving soon, and it would be her and Mr. Graber on their own again.

Which had been the plan all along, hadn't it?

"It's *oll recht*," she replied. "Samuel's visit may be the kind of healing and motivation your *daed* needs."

"You never stop caring, do you?"

As he asked the question, he startled her by suddenly moving closer and staring into her eyes. That was all it took for her heartbeat to quicken. He leaned forward and held his hand up to her face.

Was he about to pull her closer? And possibly—she couldn't believe it—kiss her?

All at once, her lungs filled with both shock and a surprisingly sweet anticipation.

"Zach?" She couldn't help but question.

"Hold still, Leah. There's a dot of paint right above your eyelashes. Can you close your eyes?"

She seriously wanted to roll her eyes for imagining he had romantic intentions. Instead, she followed his instructions. Still, she held her breath as he stepped even nearer. And felt the undeniable warmth of his fingertip gently cross over her eyelid.

"There," he whispered. "Got it. You can open your eyes now."

Slowly, she lifted her lids and found she was peering into his deep blue orbs. Those eyes her cousin had likened to the stirring depths of the ocean.

Catching herself, she blinked, then made a show of searching his face. "I was just seeing if you had any paint on you," she fibbed.

"Do I?"

"*Nee*. You're fine."

"I guess we'd better get back to work then. We're running out of time."

She nodded, and after coating their brushes with paint, they both returned to their spots along the porch again. As she ran the brush up and down over the railing, she couldn't stop thinking that Zach was wrong.

She did care what people thought. Certain people anyway. In fact, for some reason, more than ever, she was beginning to care what Zach thought about her. Mostly because he was the first man in forever that she was beginning to trust. Unfortunately, he was also a man who would soon be departing from her life.

Zach was thankful for his father's sake and everyone else's that the early evening temperature had dropped into the midseventies for their outdoor birthday celebration. As he glanced up and down the length of the folding tables covered in cream-colored tablecloths, he noticed that Leah had guessed correctly about the amount of food that they'd need. The meat platter and casserole dishes were close to empty. The deviled eggs and salad that Catherine and Anna had brought had also been a hit. And overall, he had a full, near-to-aching belly to prove it.

Beyond the food, from the grins on faces, it appeared everyone was enjoying the celebration. Amid the chatter and laughter, before Zach knew it, a wave of sentimentality washed over him, sinking him deeper into his seat. It was a feeling of family and one that he knew couldn't last. Not since he was an outsider, merely dropping in on everyone's lives. At least, however, it was something he could gladly cherish for the moment.

As he glanced at his father seated at the head of the table, balloons tied to the back of his chair, his *daed* appeared to be less grumpy than usual and more engaged as well. That was especially true when it was time for dessert, and Leah got up to fetch the cake she'd made.

"Happy birthday, Mr. Graber. This cake is double chocolate with raspberries on top," Leah told his father as she set the plate in front of him. "I hope you like it."

"Most of your cakes are *gut*," his father replied, as Leah went to sit back down. "And you know how much I like chocolate."

"I like chocolate too," Samuel called out from the middle of the table. Then, jumping out of his seat, the child headed over to his *grossdaddi*'s side.

Zach sucked in a breath, not sure how his father would react. He sensed everyone else at the table was wondering the same thing. Conversations stopped. All was still. Eyes and ears were focused on Samuel and his grandfather. Even Jonah leaned in, appearing as curious as they all were about what was going to take place at the other end of the table. *Boppli* Lydia's chirping from her high chair quieted too.

"You say you like chocolate, *buwe*?" His father's voice was still gruff as he addressed his grandson.

"*Jah*, I do." Samuel nodded vigorously.

"Then here you go." His father took a clean spoon and swiped it across the brown icing before handing it to Samuel.

Thrilled, Samuel licked every bit of frosting before handing the spoon over. *"Danke,"* he said politely.

"You're welcome."

Sighs of relief poured out around the table, and Zach figured Samuel would be seated after that. His father looked like he'd assumed the same as he removed his eyes from Samuel.

However, Samuel didn't move an inch. He

tugged on his grandfather's arm. "*Grossdaddi*, you look alone down here. Are you lonely?"

"I guess I'm not now."

It seemed out of character for his father to smile, but he did, slightly. It was also unusual to witness his father's eyes brighten. But they did to some degree.

"May I sit in your lap and keep you company?"

"And eat cake with me too?" His father snickered.

"Uh-huh."

"That may hurt your grandfather, Samuel," Matthew interrupted. Zach knew Matthew meant to give their father an excuse to avoid the closeness.

Samuel frowned. "I don't want to hurt you, *Grossdaddi*."

"You won't."

Zach watched his father hold out his arms to help Samuel climb onto his lap. His father's expression softened so much Zach barely recognized him.

"Is this a *gut* birthday?" Samuel asked his grandfather.

Zach truly believed his father's usually stern voice quivered as he placed a tentative hand on Samuel's small shoulder. "*Jah*, it is. *Verra* good."

With that, Zach glanced across the table at Leah, and found she was already looking his way. The smile they shared bonded them in a way words never had. However, it didn't last long. His father's voice interrupted them.

"You need to cut this thing, Leah," his *daed* demanded. "We need big slices for the little ones and for me too."

"Whatever you say, Mr. Graber. I'll be glad to."

She gave Zach a quick final grin before she hopped up and rushed over to his father. And though Zach knew the closeness he was feeling with her and everyone who was there to celebrate wasn't due to last, in that moment, he decided to enjoy it and be thankful to *Gott* for it. Mostly because it happened to feel good. Almost as good—he smiled—as Leah's cake promised to be.

Zach was becoming more accustomed to the meaning behind Leah's sighs. As they sat side by side in wooden rockers on the porch, gazing out into the moonlit sky, there was no doubt the sigh he'd heard was a pleasant one. Which made him smile.

"You're thinking something nice, ain't so?" he asked.

She looked over at him, noticeably surprised. "How did you know?"

"Male intuition. We men have hunches, too, you know." He broke into a smug, playful smile.

She laughed. "Well, you're right. I was thinking how we started out our day here on the porch with paintbrushes. And here we are again, relaxing on this freshly painted porch after so many good things happened today. Why, even Samuel went to sleep easily. I was anxious he might be missing his parents."

"I'm sure he got worn out running around catching fireflies after everyone left. Once you told me they're plentiful here, I didn't feel bad about putting a few in a jar to set by his bed."

"Your *daed* turned in pretty easily too. I think he had a wonderful birthday."

"A lot of credit goes to you for that, Leah."

He meant what he said, but he was sure she'd brush off his compliment. And she did. "Nonsense. Everyone contributed to the celebration. Although, if you ask me, Samuel is the one who put the real icing on the cake."

"Hmm. I only saw him and Jonah fingering a lot of it off the cake."

She giggled. "True. But you know what I mean."

"I do," he agreed. "You were right about

Daed having the chance to be around his grandsons. He seemed happier and more alive than I think I've ever seen him."

Yet as glad as he was for his father, after watching his *daed* interact with his grandsons a kind of hurtful disappointment nagged at him too. He'd been willing it to go away, reminding himself that he was a grown man. But still, it was there.

"Now, it's just women's intuition," Leah said, interrupting his thoughts, "but that didn't sound like a pleasant sigh."

"I sighed?" He quirked a brow.

"Pretty loudly."

"Oh, I was just…" He met her eyes, and in that instant realized she'd never press him for an explanation. But somehow, he wanted her to know. She was the only one he could truly trust to know. "Tonight, when my father pulled Samuel up onto his lap, I saw how my *daed*'s entire expression changed. The way he looked at Samuel was almost loving and available. And I tried to remember when I was young…" He stopped himself.

"You were thinking you never saw your *daed* look at you that way?"

She asked so softly, so knowingly, that it took him by surprise.

"If he did, I don't remember it."

"Do you recall any good times that you shared with your *daed*?"

He took his time, thinking about the years spent under the same roof with his father. Sadly, only one memory stood out to him.

"I suppose the night of my own accident and my leaving town is still so ingrained in me, I can't think of anything else when it comes to *Daed* and me." He paused momentarily. "I sometimes wonder if that's all he remembers of us too."

"But, Zach, you're here now and making new memories, aren't you? And all the ways you're helping your *daed*, why, he's got to be grateful."

He wished everything about the situation was that simple. "You don't know what I did, Leah. It was awful." He cast his sight on the starry sky before finding the nerve to look at her. "I killed Amos. His favorite horse died because of me."

Her eyes grew wide. He half expected to see condemnation in them, but there was none. "But you just said it was an accident."

"Honestly, it was more like foolish, reckless behavior on my part. I was eighteen, and we had just buried my *mamm*, and I…" He gritted his teeth, remembering. "I was hurting. But more than that, I was angry. Angry at *Gott* for taking the only parent whom I felt loved by and who cared about me. And so angry at my father, too, for not being there for my *mamm*. The entire time she lay in bed sick and dying, he was out at the barn. He was always, always with his beloved horses. She never seemed upset by that. But I was. I'd sit by her bed and pray and hold her hand, feeling helpless. Knowing there was nothing I could do. And after my *mamm* went to be with the Lord, I wanted vengeance. I wanted to hurt my *daed* the way I was hurting."

"So you took one of his horses? The thing you thought he loved most?"

He nodded. "I took off with Amos in the black of night, pressing the horse to run faster and faster along the winding roads. I didn't know where I was going, and I didn't care to know. I was wailing and screaming, and I wanted to ride until I didn't feel pain anymore."

He lowered his head and took a deep breath, hating to say the next words out loud. "But then everything changed. All of a sudden, Amos and I weren't alone on the road. A semi-truck came out of nowhere. It blasted its horn, over and over, in warning, and—"

"Amos spooked?"

"*Jah.* So much that I got thrown off. I was

thrown to safety, Leah. Me, the one who took off into the night. But Amos…" He shook his head. "I'll never, ever forget the shrill sound he made right before the truck…"

He closed his eyes, once again working to shut out the image of the dear horse lying motionless in the middle of the road. "*Daed* was crushed, of course. More hurt than I ever intended. He wouldn't even look at me or hear how much I was sorry. I wrote a lengthy note of apology to him that night since I couldn't sleep. When I gave it to him the next morning, he wouldn't look at it. He crumpled it up before my eyes and told me what I'd done was unforgivable."

"And that's why you left?"

"Because I didn't feel like I had anything to stay for."

"But when I reached out to you, Zach, you came as soon as you could."

He took a deep breath and let it out slowly. "Time away from Sugarcreek was good in a lot of ways. Mostly I realized my *daed* and I had different ways to deal with the loss of my mother. His was to shut himself away from it. Mine was to get angry and act out. And while I may never have the relationship with *Daed* that I'd like to have, I have to at least know I tried. More than that, I need *Gott* to know I tried. When *Daed* got injured, I realized if I didn't come now, there could be a day when I'd be too late and miss the chance."

Reaching out, Leah laid her hand over his and squeezed gently. He couldn't recall when he'd known anything so comforting.

"*Gott* knows your heart, Zach. He does," she whispered without hesitation. "He will bless you."

She sounded so sure of what she was saying. What she didn't know was that having such an understanding woman sitting beside him, Zach felt like the Lord already had.

Chapter Nine

It was new to her—so new!

The sharing she'd experienced with Zach on Saturday evening was like nothing Leah had ever known before.

Even two days later, as she made her way into town and stopped at the optometrist's, securing Ivy to a hitching rail, the inconceivable thought of it was still circling, delighting and overwhelming her mind. So much so that as she picked up her eyeglasses, then headed to Sunshine Bakery for her Monday group tutoring session, it was as if her body was simply going through the motions. Meanwhile, her heart kept swelling, skipping beat after beat.

And why wouldn't it?

She'd never, ever shared so much with a man as she had with Zach in the past weeks while working together for Ivan's benefit. But now it seemed their involvement with each other had deepened even more.

She'd been so touched that he'd felt comfortable enough to unburden his past to her. She'd also felt so at ease when he walked her home that same night and even caught her by the hand when she tripped in the darkness, and he didn't let go. And when he lingered on her porch for a while, talking and sharing more, a feeling of contentment caressed her like the soft breeze of the summer night.

Of course, she reminded herself, as her cheeks warmed with both embarrassment and pleasure, Zach's attention could also be disconcerting, couldn't it? Like at worship just the day before when they'd stood on opposite sides of Simon and Martha Lapp's barn, singing a hymn. He'd caught her eye and smiled in his totally charming way. Instantly, a shiver shot right through her, causing her to bumble the lyrics. Which left her asking *Gott* to forgive her for completely losing her place in the song, while also giving Him thanks for bringing Zach into her life and possibly a reason to try to trust again.

Recalling all those moments, an uncontainable smile touched her lips as she sauntered down Sugarcreek's sidewalk and stepped through the bakery door. She guessed it must've been a broader smile than she realized by the way her cousin greeted her.

"My, don't you look like a happy *maedel.*" Cat tucked her hands into her apron pockets as she came out from behind the glass counter.

"I'm always happy to be here."

"Happy, yes. But you look as sunny as the day. Anything you want to share, cousin?" Cat gave her a questioning grin.

Leah couldn't believe Cat said the word that had been swirling in her head all morning. Before she could utter a reply, Marianne joined in on the conversation.

"If you like it so much here, I'm sure we can find a job for you," the *Englischer* quipped.

"That's okay." Leah laughed. "I'm sure I'd just be in your way. Tutoring reading is about all I'm good for."

"And I think your group session today is going to be a lot of fun for the students," Cat chimed in.

"The mothers liked the idea." Leah had been glad about that. "They feel it's a way the children can meet each other and know they're not alone in getting help, and I do too. And since Samuel is around this week, it'll also be a good activity for him."

"By the way, we have the cookies all ready.

Want to see?" Marianne crooked a finger, inviting Leah to step behind the counter.

When she'd told Cat and Marianne about her group session idea and the books that she'd gotten from the library that had somewhat of a bakery theme, they had insisted on providing a cookie treat. But when she followed them behind the counter, she'd never expected to see such an extraordinary batch of cookies lining a silver tray there. Rectangular in shape, each sugar cookie was decorated to resemble a book cover with a binding. Also, each cookie "book" had a title that was the student's name. The ladies hadn't forgotten to include one for Samuel too.

"I can't believe these cookies. You two are incredible!" Leah exclaimed. "Here I always think you ladies have outdone yourself and then you go and do something to outdo yourselves again."

"*Jah*, well, what can we say?" Cat grinned. "You're going to owe us plenty of tutoring time in the years to come."

Leah crossed her heart with her finger. "I promise. I won't forget it. The children are going to love these cookies. *Danke.* Thank you both so much for making them. Seeing their names like that, it'll make the gathering today even more special for them."

Overwhelmed by Cat and Marianne's thoughtfulness, she hugged them both. Then, while the creative pair resumed their bakery duties, she got busy rearranging tables and chairs. After placing chairs in a semicircle for her students and Samuel, she began setting up tables and seats behind that arc for the adults. As she did, she made sure there were still a couple of available tables by the front window for any customers who might drop in.

Everything was in place a little before two o'clock when mothers and their children began trickling in the door. Just like always, her stomach quivered with nervous pleasure as she waved, welcoming them. Of course, the expectation of seeing Zach with Samuel in tow caused butterflies of another kind. But ten minutes later, when everyone in the group had arrived except for the two of them, those butterflies began to flit away.

"I thought you said Zach was bringing Samuel," Cat whispered as she came over to hand Leah a bottled water.

"I did. Maybe we got our wires crossed about the time."

"Well, I know he wouldn't do that to you on purpose." Cat spoke the words so assuredly that Leah wanted to believe them to be true.

Yet, noticing the clock strike two and knowing all eyes were on her, Leah decided she couldn't wait any longer. Going over to the table, she started to reach for the library books when the door chime sounded, and all heads turned from her to watch a good-looking man make his entrance. She smiled not just at the sight of Zach, sauntering in with his straw hat in hand, but also when observing the other women. Obviously, from their reaction and the way they continued staring, his attention-getting features weren't something she'd imagined.

Alongside Zach was wide-eyed Samuel, which was no surprise. But Ivan, coming along behind the two of them on his scooter, was. In fact, seeing all three generations of Graber men joined together and wholly supporting her touched Leah to her very core. As they settled into their seats, she took the time to swallow hard, swipe her misty eyes and regain her composure. Then she got started.

"Thank you all for coming this afternoon," she said, glancing around at everyone. Samuel, of course, waved. Ivan seemed as if he was readying himself to listen and not doze off. Zach winked and offered a sweet smile.

"I thought since we are fortunate to be able to gather here at Sunshine Bakery that it might be fun to borrow books from the library that have a sort of bakery theme. So that's what I did." She held up both books. "As you can see and even read for yourself, I have *If You Give a Cat a Cupcake* and also *If You Give a Mouse a Cookie.*"

A few of the children squealed, leading her to believe they were familiar with the popular, whimsical stories.

"Now, if anyone knows the words and wants to chime in while I'm reading, feel free to. All right?" She laid the first book aside, then paused. "Oh, I almost forgot." She pulled her eyeglass case from her dress pocket. "I got a pair of glasses before I came here today. I'll be wearing them for the first time as I read to you."

She placed the taupe frames on the bridge of her nose. Why she glanced at Zach again right then, she didn't know. Until he gave her a warm nod of approval, and she realized it was just what she needed.

"All right then." She cleared her throat. "Let's get started."

The eye doctor had warned that it could take days for her eyes to adjust to her prescriptive glasses. But he'd also said that the best way to get used to them was to wear them. So even though the words were still somewhat blurred on the pages—even when the spiderweb-like shimmers shone at the outside corners of her eyes—Leah continued on.

As she held up an illustrated page for everyone to see, she looked out at all the people she cared about and prayed that her vision would get back to normal soon. So that she could keep on reading. Keep on tutoring. And, hopefully—the thought struck her as her eyes landed on Zach—so that she might have a chance to keep on sharing.

Zach knew all along that Leah had agreed to ride back to the house with Samuel and his father while he went down the road a short way to meet with a contact at the Highland Property Development Company. But he also knew he hadn't told her the complete truth about why he was going there. Feeling conflicted, when he walked into Highland and Nelson Edison greeted him wholeheartedly, he put on a friendly face that didn't entirely reflect his feelings.

"Zachary, welcome. Great to see you." Clad in navy dress slacks and a summery light blue sport coat, Nelson held out his hand.

Zach shook the man's hand politely. "Thank you for seeing me. It looks like a busy place here." At a quick glance, he could see at least a half dozen men and women typing on computers or talking on cell phones. That didn't include whoever was behind the closed office doors that extended across the back of the establishment.

"We're all about making things happen." Nelson grinned. "Listen, Randall Lightner, our company director, would like to meet you as well. He's in his office right now. Do you have time?"

"I can make time. Sure."

Nelson led the way to a large corner office suited for a company director. As soon as Zach and Nelson entered Randall Lightner's office, the slightly paunchy, balding man got up from his leather chair and reached across his desk to heartily shake Zach's hand. Once Zach and Nelson were seated in chairs opposite him, Randall sat down. Elbows propped up on his desktop, he smiled.

"Zach, I'm not going to waste your time with random niceties. I'll just tell you that we feel very fortunate here at Highland that you came to us with your queries about your father's property. You seem like an astute businessman and we welcome and appreciate that. But with that being said—"

Zach had been in countless business situations and had always dreaded hearing the word *but*. However, this time out of nowhere relief surged through him. The clashing feelings inside him began to subside. His lips even started to curve upward. Even so, attempting to remain courteous and businesslike, he deliberately furrowed his brows and spoke in a serious tone.

"Randall, I completely understand if you don't want to go through with anything right now." He didn't add that it almost felt like a blessing. "Business is iffy these days."

"What?" Randall's hands dropped onto the desk while Nelson turned his head to face Zach. "No, Zach, that isn't it at all."

"Far from it," Nelson chimed in.

"What do you mean?" Zach felt his brows crease on their own this time.

"Well, as I started to say before," Randall replied, "we are very much interested in your father's property. We've had our sights set on the land for a long time. In fact, we've already drawn up papers so you can see the offer we'd like to make."

With the tip of his fingers, Randall edged a stapled proposal across the desk. Hesitantly, Zach picked up the packet and held it in his hands, barely glancing at it. There was another issue, a very important one, that needed to be discussed before even considering the dollar amount that they were offering.

He cleared his throat. "I'd like to know what you plan to do with my family's land."

Randall and Nelson looked at each other. But it was Randall who answered. "The way the acreage is laid out, and because of the farm's location and accessibility to town, we're thinking it'd be a great place for our condominium complex development. Condos, clubhouse, tennis courts, swimming pool. You know, the works."

Of course, Zach could easily visualize why they were thinking that way. With the land's combination of rolling hills and outstretches of pastureland, who wouldn't want to live in such a scenic setting? Given the town's population, however, how quickly the new homesteads would fill up, Zach wasn't sure. But that wasn't his problem. He knew for a fact that property developers were in the business of taking the greatest risks but also, generally, they reaped the greatest rewards.

"So, you're not planning on building anything that could compete with Sugarcreek's tourist attractions or businesses? Nothing that would be detrimental to them. Is that right?"

The men stared at him, most likely wondering why he cared. But he did. Not only because he was an investor in some of the town's attractions, but also because there was no way he'd do anything that would ultimately hurt the businesses of people he'd known all his life.

"That's not what we're thinking right now." Randall waved his hand as if dismissing the idea.

"I need to know it's something you won't ever consider," Zach countered firmly. "And I have to have it in writing."

"Nelson." Randall snapped his fingers. "Go tell Ellis what we need. Ask him to draw up a paper to that effect right away."

Zach held up his hand. "I don't need it written up at this very moment. But I will need it when I come in with my father to have documents signed."

That said, he wasn't sure what else there was to say. He stood up and the two men jumped to their feet as well.

"We'll have that ready for you, Zach," Randall promised.

"*Thank you.* And thanks for your interest in my father's land. I'll need a little time to present your plans and the offer to my family."

"Of course." Randall nodded. "But don't wait too long. We're ready to move forward. If not on your father's land, then somewhere else."

"I understand," Zach replied. They weren't the only ones who wanted to get plans settled.

He wanted to get a resolution in place for his father as well.

After handshakes all around, and with Highland's proposal in hand, Zach headed outside to Sugar. But once he'd unhitched her and climbed into the buggy, he didn't make a move.

Picking up the proposal, he sifted through several pages until his eyes landed on the final dollar amount. He blinked at the number, the paper shaking in his hands. The amount was astonishingly generous, higher than he ever imagined it would be.

So…he'd done it. Everything was on course. Everything was working out as he'd hoped and planned.

Still, as he set the papers aside, took up the driving lines and headed toward the farm, he realized there wasn't a trace of happiness in his heart. Or an inkling of satisfaction or thankfulness running through his veins.

Why is that, Lord?

The kind of deal Highland proposed would mean his aging father would have a secure future without the risk of getting physically hurt again. Matthew's responsibilities would be lightened and his brother's guilt diminished. And Leah…she'd grown to mean so much to him that his heart literally ached thinking how secretive he'd been with her. Still, given the large sum of money that Ivan would acquire, even she would have to agree that the sale would be the perfect answer for his father.

Yet the even bigger question was—did he wholeheartedly believe that? While a deal with Highland solved plenty of issues, was it truly the best thing for his *daed*?

Because as he pulled into his father's driveway, the Graber Horse Farm sign didn't simply seem like a public announcement to him anymore. Truth was, when he'd said the word *family* in Randall Lightner's office, for the first time in a long time it had meaning to him. Not that all was solved and that his relationship with his father was mended. Not that they didn't still have bridges to cross. But saying the word, he'd felt something.

Recalling that feeling, he tightened the reins and halted Sugar in the middle of the gravel drive. Looking out across the expanse of his family's acreage from east to west and north to south, he tried to visualize condominiums in every direction. Tried to imagine how it would feel when everything he saw before him and around him was all torn down. When there was no longer a barn or horses or a house, nor any sign that his family's life and his father's livelihood ever existed.

And the truth was, it didn't feel good. If he

was feeling that way, wouldn't his father? Or was he only being sentimental after missing out on the past five years?

Suddenly not sure what the answer, or any answer, was, he decided to wait before mentioning the Highland proposal to his father, and he clucked at Sugar to move on. He was happily and thankfully distracted when Samuel came running out the front door.

"*Onkel* Zach, you're home," his nephew greeted him. "Leah has supper ready."

And that was the other thing, wasn't it? A selfishness he was battling with, *Gott* forgive him.

Because after spending so much time being around the horses, his family and the woman who was beginning to take up residence in his heart, he really did feel like the place was starting to seem like home.

Chapter Ten

Leah rolled over in bed and turned off her alarm clock even though it hadn't gone off yet. She didn't have a need for it this morning. For the past hour, long before pink and orange rays from the sunrise began to filter through her bedroom window, she'd been lying awake, musing about her sister and brothers.

Typically, thoughts of them would have her tossing and turning while straining to come up with something more pleasant and less upsetting to fill her thoughts. But ever since Saturday night, when Zach had confided in her about the accident that had separated him and his father, and his desire to set things right, she'd been mulling over the situation with her siblings. Strangely, when she did, every once in a great while a tiny semblance of a good memory of them crossed her mind. Were there more, she wondered, buried somewhere deep within the hurt?

True, in her situation she was the injured party just like Ivan had been. But also, as it turned out, Zach had been hurting for years as well. Was it at all possible her siblings might be feeling bad too?

If her parents were still alive, no doubt they would be devastated about the falling-out between their children. Even though the two of them were now in the Lord's arms, did they deserve to have their surviving family divided here on earth?

More than anything, it was the memory of her *mamm* and *daed* that made Leah push back the sheet and get out of bed. Hurriedly getting dressed, she brushed her hair, donned an older *kapp* that her mother had sewn for her and picked up her eyeglass case from the nightstand. Her first job, after padding into the kitchen, was usually to get the coffee started. But not so this morning. Instead, with a sense of urgency, she reached for the pen and pad of paper above the sink and settled in at the kitchen table.

Then, determined to write a letter and say what needed to be addressed before any more years slipped away, she donned her glasses and began writing.

Dear Edna, Henry and Jeremiah,
How are you?

She paused, not sure where to begin.
Maybe with the simple truth?

I know it's been a long time since we've
seen each other, but I've been thinking of
you all. Before it's much later, or too late,
I want you to know that I forgive you for
what you did to me.

Sitting back in the chair, she stared at the
words she'd written. She tried to imagine her
siblings' reaction, and it wasn't good. While
it was everything she wanted to say, no doubt
they'd perceive her message as an accusation
instead of an absolution. It would only stir up
the past once more.

Instantly crumpling up the paper, she took
out a clean piece in its place.

She sighed at the empty page.

Then, gripping the pen once more and ad-
justing her glasses in hopes of seeing better,
she started over on a different note. Maybe it
was best to only address her sister initially.

Dear Edna,
Hello! I hope things are well with you and

Daniel and your kinner. *Things here in Sugarcreek have been busy. The man I work for had a bad accident with a horse, and I was taking care of him and his property by myself, which was quite a job. But ever since his son Zach arrived from Indiana weeks ago, things have gotten better.*

Much better. She smiled inwardly as her heart warmed.

And maybe it's early to be sharing this big news, but our cousin Catherine is getting married. I sure will miss her. It's been such a blessing to have her live with me ever since the Lord took Grossmammi *to be with Him. But Catherine is engaged to a wonderful man, Thomas Lehman. We happily celebrated their engagement with ice cream, outside in the moonlight.*

If you all want to get away some time, Sugarcreek isn't a far distance to come as you know. I would love to see you and your family again. I bet the kinner *have really grown. Please say hello to our brothers for me.*

Your sister,
Leah

She looked over the words she'd written and couldn't deny that her friendly tone and invitation to visit could appear mighty strange to Edna. But, following Zach's example, she didn't want to focus on the past anymore. She hoped instead to offer a path for the possibility of a future with her siblings. In that way, the letter included everything she wanted to say.

As she folded the paper into thirds, Cat sauntered into the kitchen in her pajamas. "You're up early." She yawned.

"And I'm sorry to say I didn't get the coffee made yet." Leah winced.

"No problem." Cat grabbed the teakettle and held it under the running faucet, filling it with water to be boiled and used in the French press. "What are you doing?" Her mouth stretched into another yawn.

"Writing to my sister."

"Oh!" That news woke Cat up. She blinked, then straightened and shut off the water. "Is that a *gut* thing?"

"I guess I'll find out if and when I get a letter back from her."

More often than not, Cat was extremely nosy. Yet once in a while she was silent and respectful. Leah was glad this was one of those rare times.

"Do you want any toast and jelly?"

Cat's offer sounded good, but Leah glanced at the clock and shook her head. She had three males who were depending on her. "*Nee, danke.* I should really get to work."

Once she bravely deposited the letter to her sister in the mailbox at the end of her driveway, she hustled next door. Surprisingly, Zach, Samuel and Ivan were all seated at the kitchen table and were already enjoying breakfast.

"We're having cereal today." Samuel greeted her as soon as she walked in. "With blueberries and bananas."

"So I see." She chuckled at the boy's enthusiasm.

"And we saved a seat for you." Zach nodded to a chair across from him where a cereal bowl and spoon were waiting for her. She was pretty sure the "we" who had thought of her was him.

Happily, she sat down and helped herself to the cornflakes and fruit. "The cereal is *verra* good. I guess this means I don't have to cook breakfast anymore," she teased.

"Please don't say that," Zach pleaded.

"*Jah*, a man can only eat so much cereal," Mr. Graber added.

"We're only eating cereal so we can eat quick," Samuel informed her.

"You mean quickly," she corrected him.

"Uh-uh. Quick. Because *Onkel* Zach said I

could help feed the horses, and they like to eat early, like us." His brows creased in thought. "Since you're good at feeding us, do you want to come feed the horses too?"

The child looked so adoringly sweet, she hated to say no. But she had to decline. "I'd love to, but I can't today. Your *grossdaddi*'s house needs a good cleaning." The place had been nonstop messy with a five-year-old boy tearing through it like a never-ending tornado.

"The cleaning can wait." Ivan spoke for her. "Of course she'll go with you, Samuel."

"And you're coming too, aren't you, *Grossdaddi*?"

Leah thought it might be cute to speak up for Ivan like he had for her, but he beat her to an answer.

"Not this time. I'm going to sit on the porch and enjoy the morning."

"Pleeeease?" Samuel stretched out the word.

"Eat your cereal," Ivan replied. "The horses are waiting for you."

With that reminder, Samuel dutifully got busy slurping up the moist flakes again. Meanwhile, Leah glanced across the table at Zach, who shrugged slightly.

For sure she wished Ivan would join them. But maybe, she considered, he simply wanted some time alone. He had been joining in on a lot of the activities with his grandson, and at least he'd been coming to the table for every meal now that Samuel was visiting. All things considered those improvements were a lot to thank *Gott* for. She only hoped when Samuel left that Ivan didn't slip back into his old ways—or she might have to have his grandsons come visit more often.

And then when Zach left too…

Her stomach tightened at the unsettling thought. She nudged her spoon at the remaining flakes in her bowl, no longer much interested in eating.

Somehow Zach seemed to pick up on her discomfort.

"Everything okay?"

Seeing his concerned face, she realized once again that they did share something undeniably special. Everything inside her hoped he'd stay for a long, long time. Wasn't it foolish, however, to waste any of the time she might still have with him?

"For sure. One more spoonful and I'm ready to go whenever you boys are," she said as gaily as she could manage. Then forced herself to take one last bite.

"I thought you said this was going to be fun."

At the sound of Samuel's less-than-enthused voice, Zach stopped raking out the stall he was standing in. His thoughts turned from once again ruminating about the peculiar lack of interest his father seemed to have in horses lately, to the disappointed nephew right in front of him.

Watching the young boy toss his rake aside, plop down on a bale of hay and cross his arms over his chest, Zach felt a smile twitch his lips. Oh, hadn't he felt the same way plenty of times when cleaning stalls at Samuel's age?

Sometimes he still did.

"You don't think cleaning up and helping the horses is fun?"

"The horses ain't even in here to see me do it. They ate, and then you let them go outside and play." Samuel pouted.

Zach heard Leah cough slightly. He knew her well enough by now to know she was working to stifle a chuckle. He glanced over at her and she raised her hand as if his nephew's response had outwitted them both.

"Samuel's right, Zach. It's not fair the horses get to have all the fun."

Zach was almost sure that it was harder for Leah to stop in the middle of a job than it was for him. But if she was willing… He laid his rake against the stall.

"What is it you want to play, young man?"

A smile burst across his nephew's face,

and Samuel bounced up from the bale of hay. "Hmm…" He tapped his forefinger on his chin—something Zach had seen Samuel's father do quite a few times—and looked all around. Left to right, right to left, then down and up, where Samuel's gaze stayed.

"I can go up there." His nephew pointed to the hayloft. "I'll climb up and then jump off, and you can try and catch me."

"Uh, I think not," Zach replied without a moment's hesitation.

Undaunted by Zach's response, Samuel bent over the hay bale, starting to push it across the floor.

"What are you thinking now, Samuel?" Although Zach could guess.

"If you don't want to catch me, then I can jump down and fall onto the bale of hay."

"Again, a big *nee*."

"And I second that no," Leah piped up quickly. Zach noticed how she instantly paled at Samuel's idea. "I have a way better suggestion. How about we play hide-and-seek?"

"Yay!" His nephew clapped his hands while bouncing up and down. "You two hide. I get to be 'it' first."

Right away, Samuel turned and leaned against a shelf post. Covering his eyes, he began counting. "One…two…three…"

At least he was counting slowly, which was a good thing. But not slowly enough for Zach to get his bearings. Apparently, Leah was caught off guard as much as he was, turning in circles trying to decide on a place to hide. At last they hurriedly started off in opposite directions and knocked right into each other in the process. Zach cringed when he felt her foot crunch under his.

"Six…seven…eight…" Samuel recited.

Leah was hopping up and down, holding her foot, by the time Samuel got to nine. Zach pulled her into the nearest stall with him and shut the door as quickly and quietly as he could. They both slunk down onto the hay-covered floor so they wouldn't be seen. He could tell she was in pain and trying her best not to show it.

"Are you *oll recht*?" he whispered. "I'm so sorry I stepped on your foot."

"It'll be fine." She stretched out her leg from underneath her and took off her sandal. "I know better than to wear flip-flops in here." She rubbed at her foot.

"Especially when you're with a clod like me." Feeling sorry, he dared to take a closer look. "I think I broke the skin some."

"You think so?"

She leaned to take a closer peek, but he

could tell she couldn't see what he was talking about. Maybe she needed her glasses? Without thinking, he took her foot into his hand and gently stroked a line across the scraped, reddened skin. "It's right here. Again, I'm sorry, Leah."

All at once, she began to giggle, and rapidly put a hand over her mouth.

"Did that tickle?"

"A little." She nodded. "But it's also…well, mostly, I think it's funny we're sitting here like this, hiding in a horse stall of all things. Fortunately, it's one that's been cleaned."

"Praise the Lord!" He bit back a chuckle.

"And here you are holding my foot while there's a young one out there who is keeping us all afoot."

He did laugh at that.

"I have to say, this wasn't on my to-do list today." She grinned, brushing strands of hay from the lap of her skirt.

"I hear you. But what's even funnier, Leah, is that right now…"

He stopped himself, not sure if he should say what he was feeling. But then, as always, her warm, beautiful, guileless eyes seemed to beckon him, letting him know he could say whatever was on his mind. Which meant he couldn't seem to stop himself from sharing what was in his heart. "Being here with you, I can't think of another place that I'd rather be," he uttered softly.

Everything about her reaction told him she felt the same. The way she didn't move an inch away and yielded toward him. How she smiled shyly, irresistibly, and lifted her chin. The way she seemed to be waiting on him.

And so he cupped her chin tenderly. Then he inclined his head and drew closer... When abruptly, she pulled back and sat up straight, her hazel green eyes wide.

"Zach!" she exclaimed, her excited tone confusing him.

"What?"

"Samuel!"

"Samuel? Where?" He glanced around them, every which way.

Leah clasped his cheek and turned his face toward hers. "He never said 'ready or not, here I come.' What if he—"

She didn't have to finish her sentence. He understood right away. "The hayloft!"

They both shot up and sprang out of the stall. Thankfully, they could see in an instant that Samuel was on solid ground. With his back turned toward them, he stood emptying out a wooden box he'd found on one of the shelves behind the post. At his feet were a few other containers that he'd noticeably rummaged through.

"I thought you were going to come look for us."

"I was, but you made it too easy. I could hear you laughing right over there." He nodded toward the stall they'd been in. "Then I started to look through *Grossdaddi*'s boxes, and I found a horse. I was looking to see if there was more of them."

"What do you mean, a horse?" Zach was confused.

"A horse like this."

Samuel picked up a carved wooden horse from the bale of hay he'd been sitting on earlier and handed it to Zach. Gripping the football-sized piece in his hand, Zach could see that it was high quality, despite being covered with streaks of grimy dust.

"I think it's been playing hide-and-seek too," Samuel said. "Can I have it since I found it?"

"I can't say, Samuel. That's a question for your *grossdaddi*." Zach turned the horse in his hands, admiring the details. "It's beautifully made. It might be something special to him."

"I wonder if someone in town made it?" Leah asked curiously.

"Good question." He rotated the carving, wiping away smudges of dirt here and there.

"Oh." He noticed some letters. "Let's see, it says—"

Stunned, he stared at the initials, tongue-tied. Then he held the horse closer, eyeing the letters all over again, not believing what he was seeing.

"Zach, what is it?" Leah's concerned voice reverberated in his ears. "You look shocked."

"Are you okay, *Onkel* Zach?" Samuel stepped closer.

"*Jah*, it's just…just so strange to see this." He looked up at them both. "The initials are I.G."

Chapter Eleven

"I.G.? Your *daed*?"

Leah didn't mean for her tone to sound so incredulous. But she was as astonished as Zach seemed to be that his *daed*, of all people, had sculpted such an impressive piece of art. Even more, she was trying to get her bearings and her head on straight after the almost-kiss from Zach.

"Take a look for yourself." Zach held the upside-down horse for her to see. Squinting, she still couldn't quite make out the letters.

"I believe you. It's just that sitting down quietly and being patient enough to carve something that beautiful seems so un—"

Realizing Samuel was looking up at her and hanging on every word, she halted right there. It wouldn't be right to say anything negative about his grandfather. Even if the art of wood carving did seem to be an unlikely and unfit match for the brusque man she knew and cared so much for.

"Leah, you didn't finish saying *un* what," Samuel spoke up, not letting her off the hook.

She began to stammer. Thankfully, Zach came to her rescue. "I think Leah was about to say it seems so *unbelievable* that your grandfather or anyone could create such a beauty as this. Right, Leah?"

"*Jah*, absolutely." She bobbed her head in agreement.

"Can we take it to *Grossdaddi* and show him I found it? Or do we have to rake more?"

Zach didn't hesitate to answer. "I say we put away the rakes and head back to the house."

After the rakes got hung, they hustled outside. A few minutes later, Leah was glad to see Ivan was still seated on the porch right where they had left him, enjoying the sunshine.

"You're back so soon?" he called out.

"I found something hiding in the barn, *Grossdaddi*."

Samuel darted up the steps ahead of her and Zach, positioning himself next to Ivan's chair.

"You did? Was it a mouse? Or a garter snake?" Ivan hissed. "Or did a rabbit get in there?"

"Nee." Samuel shook his head. "It was a horse."

Ivan chuckled, his face lighting up merrily. "Well, of course, you found horses in the barn, grandson. That's no mystery."

"He's talking about this horse, *Daed.*"

Zach had been holding the carving at his side. When he lifted it and handed it to his father, Leah saw the amusement instantly fade from Ivan's eyes.

"Oh, *jah.* This," was all he said, grasping it loosely.

"Daed, you act like the carving is nothing special. It's a work of art. I can't believe I never knew—"

His father cut him off. "Because it was something you didn't need to know," he replied before addressing his grandson. "Samuel, why don't you take this horse and go inside and have some cookies and lemonade." He held out the carving to Samuel, who grabbed it right away.

"I can help him," Leah spoke up. She wasn't sure what had made Ivan's mood shift so quickly. She also wasn't sure she wanted to know and began to follow Samuel toward the screen door.

"He doesn't need your help." Ivan stopped her. "Do you, Samuel?"

"Horse will help me." The child smiled before romping inside.

Leah hated to see Samuel go since he had been the only one of them smiling. She was sure she looked bewildered, and Zach's features had crumpled into a disgusted expression.

"You're talking in riddles, *Daed.*" Zach immediately pounced on his father. "What do you want to leave me out of this time? What didn't I need to know?"

Watching Ivan's lips tighten and hoping to calm Zach before the two of them sparred verbally, she placed a gentle hand on Zach's shoulder.

Ivan answered gruffly, "You didn't need to know that I carved that horse for your sister."

Taken aback, Leah's mouth dropped. Apparently shocked as well, Zach collapsed onto the end of the empty porch chair. "But...but I don't have a sister." He began shaking his head. "Do I?"

"You would've," Ivan said succinctly and solemnly.

"I don't know what you mean," Zach replied. Leah was lost as well.

"You would've had an older sister, but the Lord took her right after she was born. I'd made that horse for her and was going to surprise your *mamm* with it, but never did." He paused and let out a long, weary breath. "I don't know why I didn't throw it away instead of hiding it. Maybe it was my way of holding on to that *boppli* girl."

"It's beautiful, *Daed*." Leah heard Zach's voice soften.

"Verra," she added.

Ivan eyed them both and smiled slightly. "So was she," he said wistfully.

"Was that horse the first thing you ever carved?"

"The first thing that meant anything to me."

"Well, *Daed*, you certainly have a gift for sculpting, a really special talent." Zach leaned toward his father. "Have you ever thought about doing more of it?"

"I've done a little here and there," Ivan answered indifferently.

"Well, you could be like Leah," Zach insisted.

Her head jerked at that. "Like me?"

"Jah, you're using your gifts by caregiving and tutoring, ain't so?"

She didn't respond, not very comfortable with him drawing attention to her. Thankfully, he turned back to his father.

"And your wrist seems to be a lot better now, *Daed*."

"That doesn't matter much. It's my right wrist that got sprained, and I'm left-handed."

"Oh, that's right." Zach smiled. "Even better."

"Some of the world's greatest artists like Leonardo da Vinci and Michelangelo were left-handed," Leah couldn't resist adding.

"See, there you go." Zach chuckled. "I'd be happy to buy you a set of carving knives or whatever it is you use."

"I don't need anything like that." Ivan shook his head. "I have a set stored away."

"I say it's time to get them out then."

"Ach!" Ivan waved a hand, dismissing the idea. "If it's time for anything, it's time for my lunch," he countered. "Isn't that right, Leah?"

She glanced back and forth between the opposing men. At Zach, obviously a man who wanted to do the best for others, whose expression was marked with a kind but very determined earnestness. And then at Ivan, who had a mind of his own and rarely seemed to like suggestions, especially when they had something to do with him.

Maybe a noonday meal really would be the simplest answer for their stalemate.

"I'm happy to get lunch for all of us," she replied. "How about egg-salad sandwiches?"

That seemed like something the pair could

agree on, and she started for the door. Yet as she took one step in front of the other, the path didn't seem so open and clear. Puzzled, she tried to understand what was happening. Yes, she'd been dealing with the shimmering at the corners of her eyes, but now those tendrils of light had turned somewhat shadowy. Which didn't make sense. Hadn't the doctor just diagnosed her as farsighted with slight astigmatism?

Then why did it feel like the world was closing in on her?

Especially, at a time like this in her life when her heart was beginning to open up?

In the early evening, Zach stood in the doorway of his father's bedroom, surprised by his *daed* for the second time that day. Never had he seen his father appear so comfortable and, more than that, so caring. The man was asleep, all snuggled in bed with his dozing grandson leaning against him. Samuel was still hugging the carved horse to his side while his grandfather held him close.

Earlier, Zach had heard Samuel's voice as his nephew partly read and mostly spoke his way through a favorite children's book. Now the book lay open on the bed. Samuel hadn't made it to the last page. No doubt the day had left the two of them tired but obviously completely content with one another. They'd drifted off to sleep.

"Isn't that the sweetest thing you've ever seen?"

Zach caught a whiff of Leah's flowery shampoo as she leaned over his shoulder and whispered in his ear.

"It really is," he agreed. He couldn't remember as a child when he'd ever cuddled with his father that way. Those times were always reserved with his *mamm*. Still, it was a heartwarming sight and proof again that his father did have a heart.

"It's precious to see." Leah echoed his thoughts. "Want me to help you put Samuel in his own bed?" she asked.

"Not yet. They look too content like that, and this is Samuel's last night here. I'll move him a little later. I promise."

They turned and went into the kitchen, which he'd helped Leah clean up after dinner. It was then he remembered another promise he'd made. He grabbed an apple from the fruit bowl on the table.

"Are you still hungry?"

"*Nee*. I promised Bear an apple earlier and told him I'd be back with one." He twirled the piece of fruit in his hand. "Would you want to go with me?"

She leaned over and picked up two more apples from the green-trimmed bowl and tucked them into her apron pockets. "Better take some extras for the others, just in case."

"I guess that's a yes then?" He cocked his head.

"It is." She smiled up at him.

The sun had lowered in the sky but still cast a golden glow over the fields as they made their way to visit the horses. With Leah by his side, Zach caught himself thinking that he felt as if he was glowing too. After almost kissing her earlier in the day, he was thankful she didn't seem shy or uncomfortable being with him. As they leaned against the fence gazing at the sleek-coated horses in the pasture, their shoulders brushed against each other, and she didn't seem to mind that either.

"Bear looks like he's found some friends out there," she said. "You brought him around pretty quickly."

"Now I'm wondering if I've made him so comfortable that he's off with his horse buddies and has forgotten about me."

"Oh, now." Leah giggled. "I bet parents think that about their children sometimes too." She gave his shoulder a friendly pat. "Apparently you've done well with him, Zach, and made him feel at ease and trusting with the three steps I told you about. You spent time with him, created a positive association so he thinks of you as a calming presence. And you've learned his likes and dislikes." She nodded to the apple in his hand.

"I also discovered he likes to have his nose rubbed. Not so much his mane as his nose. Aren't you proud of me?"

"Oh, now, pride goes before a fall," she quipped, teasingly. "But I do think knowing those kinds of things about Bear has made you closer to him, ain't so?"

"I do. And… I think it works for humans too."

"I never thought of it like that, but I suppose it could."

He watched her brows knit together as if considering what he'd said which gave him the courage to go on.

"It does. Take you and me, for instance."

She turned completely and looked up at him, a curious smile curving her lips. "You and me?"

"*Jah.* I now know after buying many pints of the wrong flavors of ice cream that pineapple sherbet is your favorite from Dipsy Do's."

"That was an expensive trip to the ice cream shop that night, wasn't it?"

Her words were somewhat apologetic, but her eyes sparkled with amusement. He wanted to tell her he'd spend any amount of money to put a smile on her face. But he kept that to himself. "*Jah*, but it was worth it. That was a special night."

"With the engagement announcement, you mean?"

"That, and you and I had a chance outside of our workday to get to know each other better. We had a—what do you call it? A positive association. I liked that."

"Me too." She tilted her head, giving him a coy grin. "So…what else do you know about my likes and dislikes?"

"Ah, that's easy. I know that you enjoy reading books by the creek. You love opening the eyes and minds of children. I know that, like it or not, you can't help caring about everyone else more than yourself. And the biggest thing—" He paused dramatically, knowing that would stir her interest even more. Which it did.

"What?" She poked at his shoulder. "Tell me."

"I know your favorite breakfast foods and that you're *verra, verra* jealous of my sausage gravy and biscuits."

Hearing her raspy, wholehearted laughter brought him great joy.

"I wouldn't say I'm jealous exactly. I'm more like amazed. And if you'd ever share the recipe with me, I bet I could make both of those as good as you."

"You do, huh?" He quirked a playful brow. "Let me tell you, the secret is not in the ingredients. Trust me, it's in the way I fix those dishes."

"Well, come to think of it, that could be true. Besides making a great breakfast, you grill up the best barbecued ribs that I've ever tasted too."

"So you liked those, huh?" He was enjoying the compliments that came from her.

"Liked them? I loved them."

"Why, *danke*. I like plenty of things you cook too."

"Or things that I bake, like my *grossmammi*'s chocolate chip cake. I know that's one of your favorites, along with any flavor of ice cream that Dipsy Do's has to offer. But more than that, I think I know what's most dear to your heart."

Hearing her speak those last words, he couldn't tear his gaze from her. Did she have any idea how important she was becoming to him?

"You are a fixer, Zachary Graber," she continued. "And not just an all-around handyman sort of fixer, which comes totally naturally to you. But you also like to fix everything and everyone around you. It seems to be your greatest desire for everyone to be their best and happiest. And when you're having trouble fixing something, I've seen that you don't stop and say that you can't. No, you keep at it, trying to find another way."

He was so moved that he could barely speak.

"And what you've done for your *daed* so far, Zach," she went on, "may not appear like much to you. But it is. Also, I know right now it seems like he doesn't want to be around the horses much."

"You've noticed that too?" Was she beginning to see things about his father like he did? That would surely make things easier. A wave of thankfulness washed over him—until she spoke again.

"I have. But I imagine he's only frustrated, knowing that he can't care for them yet the way that he used to. But I don't believe for a minute that it means he doesn't love them anymore. This place has been his life. The horses have been his life." Realizing what she'd said, she cringed. "I'm sorry. I didn't mean that the way it came out."

"It's fine. I admit, when I first got here, I

would sit on this fence and think what a great load of work those creatures were." He closed a hand over the wooden rail, remembering. "But after caring for them and getting to know them better, they've sure grown on me."

"And when your *daed*'s ready, you'll have everything in place for him. Healthy, happy horses and a farm and house that are in better shape than they've been for a very long time."

Guilt poked at the pit of his stomach. He had to look away from the trust and admiration in her eyes. Blindly staring out into the pasture, he felt everything inside him was at war. He needed to come clean and tell her about Highland's offer. But why bring up something he wasn't completely settled on himself? Or was he? He'd hidden the proposal in a bottom drawer of his dresser. But he hadn't stopped taking it out and looking at it every now and then. Some days he wanted to share the offer with her to get her opinion. Other days he prayed she didn't come across the paper and think the worst of him for considering it as an answer for his father.

"Zach." She laid a hand on his forearm, interrupting his thoughts. "I hope I didn't embarrass you. Those aren't just offhanded compliments. It's all true."

"Leah—" He squeezed her hand, unable to

hold back from her any longer. "I've been try-ing to find a way to—"

"Zach, I know you have. You've not only tried to find a way for your *daed*." Her inno-cent eyes searched his. "You're making a way for him. Oh, and there's something I've been meaning to tell you all day. Because of your example in attempting to make amends with your *daed*, I wrote a letter to my sister this morning in hopes I can do the same thing."

"You did? I hope I didn't say anything to make you think you had to do that."

"Not at all. But you know what? It has been a long day, and suddenly my head is pound-ing. I should go."

"How about I get the horses inside quickly? Then I'll walk you home." In a way, he was happy to have the day end as well.

"*Nee*. I'll be fine. But you should take these." She emptied the apples from her apron pock-ets, handing them to him. "And you should stay since you made a promise to Bear. Be-cause that's another thing I know about you."

Cupping the extra apples in his hands, he was baffled. "What's that?"

"You're a man who doesn't like to break his promises." She smiled up at him. "I'll see you in the morning, okay?"

"Bright and early, I hope." He nodded.

"Of course," she said softly.

Once she left his side and walked away, guilt not only poked at Zach again. It stabbed, long and hard. As he scanned the wide-open sky, brilliantly lit with the glimmering colors of sunset, all the beauty was lost on him. Instead, he bowed his head, closed his eyes, trying to unburden his heart. He prayed, asking the Lord to help him find a way to be the man Leah thought him to be. He prayed, knowing *Gott* was better at keeping promises than he'd ever be.

Chapter Twelve

It was Samuel's last day at Ivan's house. Leah was leaning over the guest bed, packing the child's suitcase with freshly laundered clothes, when Zach walked into the bedroom.

Coming alongside her, Zach held up one of his nephew's socks and a short-sleeved shirt as well. "You dropped these in the hallway."

"Oh, I did? *Danke.* I was wondering where they'd gone to."

She deliberately barely glanced at Zach while taking the sock and shirt from his hands. The way her eyes had been acting up all morning, she was afraid there might be something in them he would see. Instead, she focused on intently folding the shirt and locating the sock's mate before adding the items to the luggage just so. But even without looking at Zach, she sensed him watching her thoughtfully.

"Leah, you seem somewhat off balance today. Do you still have your headache from last evening?" he asked sympathetically.

A flash of heat leaped up her neck at his question. For sure, she didn't want to lie to him, but she was also simply trying to get by and didn't want to think about the struggle she'd been going through. From the moment she'd opened her eyes that morning, a shock wave of fear bolted through her leaving her nauseated in its wake. The weblike spots that had occasionally been clouding her peripheral vision—the ones she'd been praying would fade away—were worse than ever before. Overnight it seemed those wispy images had turned into a wall of darkness. Like a horse with blinders on, she could barely see out the sides of her eyes.

Was she truly going blind like the aenti *Cat had mentioned?*

Her insides quaked at the terrifying thought, and she struggled to appear calm. "I've just been busy, trying to get a lot done before you take Samuel home later. I didn't want to send him back with soiled clothes for Anna to wash. I'm sure she's exhausted after spending the week with her sister's newborn twins."

"And that's why you made the potpie for their family too?"

"And one for you and Ivan."

"And you're sure you're not trying to avoid me? Because it seems like you are."

His voice was flooded with so much concern that she couldn't resist looking at him. She turned her head in order to see his face fully.

"Did I say something last night that might've offended you?" He dipped his head slightly.

Offend her? She was falling for him even more with his charmingly sweet comments about her likes and dislikes. And as far as avoiding him, she was simply hoping that if she just kept busy and tried to do everything that she always did, then her eyes would get back to doing their job too. She needed to keep going, after all, for the people in her life who depended on her.

Yet gazing up at him, her heart wrenched knowing that she wasn't sharing the way she'd become accustomed to doing with him. But what was there to share except for something she didn't understand herself?

"Not at all, Zach. I had a *gut* time with you. I always do."

If she didn't know better, it seemed those simple words had the broad-shouldered, six-foot man grinning widely as if she'd made his day.

"Then you'll come with me and Samuel to the creek? Ivan doesn't feel comfortable joining us because it's too far and too uneven a path. But it's Samuel's last time for a while, and he wants you to go."

"Oh, I don't know…" She understood Ivan's trepidation perfectly. With the way her eyes were behaving, she was somewhat intimidated by the walk as well.

But before she could give a definite answer, Samuel came bursting into the room. "Please come to the creek, Leah. Pleeeease." He elongated the word, typical for him.

Looking down at his dear, earnest face, she caved and held up her hands in surrender. "You're irresistible, you know that?"

"What does that mean?" Samuel asked.

"Don't worry, nephew," Zach answered. "It's a good thing, and I'm happy to say it means yes."

Minutes later, the three of them left Ivan in the sitting room staring at a puzzle that he and Samuel had started. It was another activity she'd never seen him engage in prior to his grandson's visit. Still, she had to wonder how much he'd truly work on it once Samuel was gone. Already, he seemed listless and kept mentioning Samuel's departure throughout the morning. She wished she knew of something positive to lift his spirits. But it had taken so much of her energy to simply put one foot in front of the other and not give in to her tunnel vision that she hadn't found the answer.

Fortunately, Zach didn't seem to notice or mind her unhurried gait as he sauntered beside her in the glare of the midday sun. However, Samuel was too excited about their outing to take things slowly. He romped ahead of them. The golden-haired boy already had his shoes off, and his trouser legs curled up, by the time she and Zach reached the creek.

While Zach joined his nephew in the water, she happily settled on the grassy bank. Though it shouldn't have felt like such an accomplishment, she was mighty thankful she'd made the walk without falling or tripping. As silly as it would've seemed just days ago, she let out a sigh of relief. Ready to relax, she removed her shoes and dipped her feet into the welcoming water. Then, leaning back on her elbows, she closed her eyes.

In a strange way it was comforting not to have to worry about what she might not be seeing. As the sun warmed her face, she tried her best to shut out thoughts and worries that might leave her feeling cold. For everyone's sake on Samuel's last day, she needed to pretend that all was well with the world. And for her own sake, she needed to think that, too, even for just a moment.

The nervous tension that had gripped every muscle in her body since dawn was just beginning to slacken when the sound of Zach's voice jolted her.

"Ready, Samuel?" he shouted.

"*Jah!*" Samuel squawked.

Her eyes shot open, not sure what was about to happen. Deftly, as if they'd practiced it, the pair jumped out of the creek. Zach clasped her right hand while Samuel grabbed her left. She hardly had a chance to resist as they pulled her into the stream.

"What are you doing? You're not going to dunk me, are you?"

"*Nee.* We're taking you wading." Samuel giggled, which delighted her so much she found herself laughing.

"Oh, you are, huh?"

"*Jah*, isn't that what we came for?" Zach's eyes never appeared bluer or felt warmer as he readjusted his clasp and intertwined his fingers with hers.

Without a free hand to hike up her skirt, her hem was getting drenched. Even so, she couldn't care less. Holding on tight, she was too caught up in the fun. Too overjoyed to be skipping and squealing through the water with two people so close to her heart.

Although, she wasn't surprised by any

means when Samuel suddenly let go. A young boy, bent on experiencing everything he could, he splashed around the creek bed on his own. Meanwhile, Zach must've thought the adults had waded enough. She didn't mind when he led her to a shale ledge for them to sit on. Lifting her skirt out of the water, she wrung out the hem in her hands and sighed.

"Now that sigh is one that I'm not so sure about." He gave her a puzzled look. "Is it happy or sad?"

She gave him a slight smile, not sure herself. It took a moment to find the answer. "I'd say thankful."

His brows rose. "For?"

"Thankful to you for pulling me out of..." Her mood? Her fear? She wasn't yet ready to share about that, and it wasn't what she was feeling anyway. Was it? More than drawing her away from something, he'd brought her nearer. Being close to him and Samuel had awakened a hint of joy in her. "For pulling me in, I mean."

"It was Samuel's idea."

She raised her brows, giving him a knowing smile. "Oh, I doubt that."

"Well, let's say I didn't have any trouble getting him to go along with me."

She laughed. "Well, it felt mighty good, Zach. I needed it."

"I'm glad."

The genuineness was unmistakable not only in his voice but his gaze. As his eyes captured hers, he reached toward her face. She recalled plenty of times when she'd witnessed his powerfully strong hands perform plenty of heavy-duty tasks. Yet as he slowly tucked a strand of her fallen hair back into her *kapp*, his touch was so gentle, so soft, it nearly made her gasp.

She was just as breathless when his hand drifted down to take hold of hers. He covered her palm with his warmth, and his clasp lingered as if taking claim. Yet sadly, as much as she wanted to bask in the feeling of his affection, the still-small voice of her conscience wouldn't let her rest.

Oh, how she needed to be honest with him for his sake and hers. Even at the risk of losing whatever the undeniable attraction was between them, she knew she had to speak up.

And I will, she promised herself. *I will*. But not on Samuel's last day. It simply wasn't the time or the place.

That was unmistakably true when Samuel suddenly came in search of a playmate.

"*Onkel* Z!" he called out, and Zach turned to look. The next thing she knew, Samuel's small hands were lapping up the water, trying to fling it in Zach's direction. Of course, it was all to get his uncle's attention. Zach tuned in to that right away.

Delicately letting go of her hand, Zach raised both of his in the air.

"I'm going to get you!" He growled like an angry ogre as he took off after his nephew. That had Samuel squealing and trying to tread through the water as quickly as he could. Zach could've caught up with him in two long strides but kept up his surly act and distance while taking his time.

Finally, a few yards down the stream, he reached out and yanked his nephew from the creek water. Flinging him over his shoulder, Zach grunted and heaved while Samuel dangled down his uncle's back, shrieking merrily.

And suddenly, she was overwhelmed.

She was overcome by the sound of Samuel's laughter and the exuberance of his smile. Moved by the joyful pleasure on Zach's face and the way he held the boy so protectively and lovingly. And it was all happening within the rippling water under the expanse of a cloudless, blue sky. While a pair of bright red cardinals chirped happily from a tree limb, appearing as if they might want to join in on the fun. Which didn't seem to be the case with a cluster of fluttering, yellow-winged butterflies who seemed too engrossed in furry tips of cat-tails and violet irises to be bothered.

Oh, how much longer would she be able to see it all? The joy. The beauty. And—sadness gripped her heart at the thought—the look of affection she'd seen in Zach's eyes?

Soon, would it all only be a memory?

Is that what was happening to her?

An aching from deep inside gnawed at her. Already, she was beginning to miss everything and everyone she knew. Unable to control her emotions, tears flowed unceasingly from her eyes. The same eyes that threatened to enclose her world in darkness. She stood up abruptly, her skirt hem dropping into the water again. Slushing quickly through the stream, she has-tened up the bank and grabbed her shoes.

Not even bothering to slip them on, she hugged them to her chest and began walking away from everything within her sight.

"Leah?" Zach's startled voice called after her. "Leah!" he shouted more vehemently.

She didn't want to stop and face him even though he kept calling her name.

"Leah, wait! Please stop."

Zach jumped out of the water and stood on the bank, calling after her, feeling more con-founded than he'd ever been in his life. He thought they'd shared a moment. He thought there was something special between them. He thought they'd grown so close and now with tears running down her cheeks, she was walking away. And wouldn't even turn to look at him. What had he done? What was happening?

Everything in him wanted to run after her but he was afraid approaching her would only chase her farther away.

"Leah, please, how can I help? What's wrong?"

At first, he didn't think she was going to answer him. Finally, after a distance, she turned to face him.

"Nothing," she said simply, swiping at the tears that proved otherwise.

"Nothing? I'm not stupid, Leah. I don't think you're crying because of nothing."

"Girls do sometimes. At least this girl does. If you don't like it, well, then…" She sniffed, shrugging her shoulders indifferently. Causing him to gape at her.

Where was this coming from? It didn't even sound like her. Was she trying to anger him, push him away? Well, it wasn't going to work.

"Leah." He deliberately softened his voice. "I'm ready to listen. If I did something wrong, you just have to say so."

His plea caused another surge of tears to

stream down her face. Did that mean she was touched by his words? Or irritated by his concern?

Completely perplexed, he rubbed his forehead not knowing what else to say. Samuel stepped out of the water and leaned against his leg, seeming to be confused too.

"Are you sad that I'm leaving, Leah?" his nephew asked innocently. "Is that it?"

Leah's eyes clouded again, and Zach prepared himself for more tears. But then her lips slowly crimped into a slight smile.

"*Jah*, sweet *buwe*. You guessed it."

A light chuckle made its way through Leah's tears and she opened her arms. Samuel wasn't hesitant about running over and stepping into her embrace.

"It's okay," his nephew said soothingly. "I'll come back soon."

"You'd better."

It was comforting for Zach to hear Leah chuckle again. But noticing how she thumbed his nephew's soft cheek, then scanned Samuel's face as if seeing it for the last time, he was bewildered once more.

What is going on with her, Lord? Why the sudden change?

"Leah, we're walking you home. I want to make sure you get back safely."

"*Nee.*" She held up her hand. "It's all right." She sniffled. "Just a headache again. Probably from the heat. I need to rest is all."

"You have done a lot of work today."

"For sure. But never mind me. This is Samuel's last day and you two should keep up your game until it's time for you to take him home."

"Can we, *Onkel*?" Samuel immediately turned to him. "Will you pretend to be a monster again?"

Zach was about to decline, but Leah answered for him. "*Jah*, he will. You two enjoy yourselves." She shooed Samuel his way. "And don't forget to take Samuel's suitcase and the potpie when you leave later."

"We won't," Samuel shouted as he latched onto Zach's hand and Zach reluctantly let himself be tugged back toward the water.

"Leah, I'll check on you after I get back from town," Zach promised.

"No need to, Zach. Really, I'll be fine."

As she stepped away and Samuel pulled him back into the creek, Zach wished he could be hopeful that she would be fine. And that the two of them together would be too. Yet doubt crept into his heart and mind. Everything inside him wasn't believing that.

"*Onkel* Z, you need to start growling at me again," Samuel insisted. "Like before."

Zach did as his nephew requested even though his heart wasn't in it. In fact, his heart felt sick and it had appeared Leah was feeling the same way too. If only he knew the reason why. Maybe he could fix it?

Staggering back to her house, Leah knew the moisture from her tears was blinding her path even more. But she couldn't help herself. Her heart broke again and again, hating to leave Zach looking so beside himself. The deception was hurting her something awful too. Obviously, the man knew her well enough to know she was hiding something from him.

I can't go on like this. I've got to tell him. And I will. As soon as I see him, I will.

With a tight grip on her porch handrail, she climbed the concrete steps. As she did, it occurred to her that this was the only time she'd ever left the creek feeling far worse than when she'd gone there.

Coming in from the bright outdoors left her vision even more shadowy than ever. Taking cautious steps into the kitchen, she leaned over the sink anxious to splash cold water on her face. Anything to help wash away the sadness. Anything to suppress the tears. Before she could turn on the faucet, she sensed something behind her and jumped into the air.

"Cat!" she gasped, her hand flying to her chest.

"I'm sorry I scared you. I thought you saw me when you came in."

"What are you doing home?" she asked.

"Don't you remember?" Her cousin gave her a puzzled look. "I only worked a half day because Thomas and I are looking for places to live today. And then I'm going to be staying with my parents tonight so I can help *Mamm* with a few things. The question is…" Her forehead crinkled. "What are you doing here? Did you and Zach have a fight or something?"

She shook her head. They'd never come close to such a thing, had they? "No, I'm just kind of headachy today."

"Oh, well…" Her cousin put her hands to her hips. "I could understand if you got into a tiff with him. Unless you've known all along what I found out this morning."

Completely thrown off, Leah blinked. "Found out what?"

"About his deal with the Highland Property Development Company."

"Oh, that." Relieved, Leah waved her hand. "It's not his deal. He told me he was going to make an inquiry with them for a friend."

Cat bit her lip. Her cousin's brows creased

in that sisterly protective way they did when she was trying to spare Leah's feelings.

"Just go ahead and say what you need to say, Cat. I'm not going to be mad at you."

"I know. It's just that Marianne's husband manages a construction company that Highland uses for most of their developments. And he said that their next project will begin when Zach forces his father to sign the papers that will turn the Graber farm into a condominium complex."

Cat said the last sentence all in a rush. Still, it took a minute for the words to sink in. When they did, they felt like a blow to her chest, making it hard for her to breathe.

"*Nee.* No." She shook her head vehemently. "That's not possible. All along, Zach and I have been working together to get Ivan and his property in shape. We've been doing it so Ivan can get back to work again. It wasn't for any other reason than that."

Cat eyed her sorrowfully. "Zach has the papers in his possession, Leah," she said softly.

Dumbstruck, Leah stumbled into the living room. With a heavy heart and weak legs, she slumped down on the couch and stared.

Oh, when it came to Zach, she'd been blind to so many things. To everything in fact. To his warm smiles. And his caring touch. And most of all, to every word uttered from his mouth.

Chapter Thirteen

"*Onkel* Zach, don't you think it would make my *mamm* happy if we stopped at the bakery and got her cookies before you take me home?"

At the sound of his nephew's voice coming from the back of the buggy, Zach was immediately upset with himself. He'd hardly said a word during the trip to take Samuel home. His mind had still been whirling nonstop, trying to figure out what had happened at the creek to upset Leah. To say he'd been distracted was putting it extremely mildly.

Which wasn't fair to his nephew, or even him, was it? After all, who knew when he'd have a chance to spend alone time with Samuel again.

Glancing over his shoulder, he put on a serious face, which, given the way he was feeling, wasn't so hard to manage.

"Hmm. Cookies for just your *mamm*? Do you think we should get some for you and for Jonah too?"

Samuel's eyes instantly grew wide, his head bobbing excitedly. "And don't forget Lydia. If she's too little to eat them, Jonah and I will eat them for her."

The boy was truly a crafty negotiator. For the first time in hours, Zach smiled. But not quite as widely as Samuel when they stopped at the bakery. The boy grinned ear to ear as they walked—more like Samuel ran—through Sunshine Bakery's door.

His nephew's eyes didn't stop gleaming as he stood in front of the brimming bakery display cases. Pointing out one cookie after another, he wasn't shy about how many he'd need of each. Samuel even insisted on picking out a dozen for Zach to take home.

By the time Marianne packed up Samuel's selections, the cookies filled two bags and two boxes. Seeing that, Zach knew Anna was likely to scold him for buying the dozens of cookies Samuel had chosen. Yet gratified that he could make at least one person in his life happy, Zach decided he'd take whatever disapproval was coming to him. However, that came quicker than he expected. He was in the process of pay-ing Marianne when he heard an older man's clucking coming from behind them.

"Young man, you're not going to eat all those cookies by yourself, are you? If so, you're sure to get a tummyache."

Zach sighed and rolled his eyes. Could anything go right today? Already the reprimands were starting, huh? Turning to see his accuser, Zach saw a familiar, friendly face instead.

"Dr. Rubin!" Zach held out his hand ready to shake with the *Englischer* whom he'd known his entire life. Before the men could perform that ritual, Samuel stepped between them.

"Do you want a cookie?" his nephew asked the gentle man.

"No, son. I'm partial to the blueberry muffins here. But thank you anyway. That's very polite of you."

"Then can I eat one now, *Onkel*?"

"*Jah*, but only one," Zach conceded. While Samuel set the treats on a table and took his time choosing, Zach was glad to be able to turn to Dr. Rubin again.

"He's very persuasive." Dr. Rubin chuckled. "Must take after your brother."

"You know, I'd never put that together. But you're right." Zach grinned.

"And how are you doing, Zach? It's good to see you."

"I'm doing well, thank you. And you?"

The kind doctor had come to the farm plenty of times during his *mamm*'s last days. Even now, Zach still felt incredibly grateful to him. The five years had changed the man some, though. His hair was whiter and there was less of it, while his middle was bulging and there was more of it. Still, the light of caring that always shone in his eyes hadn't seemed to dim.

"I'm hanging in there. Thanks for asking. Knees have been giving me trouble for years. But this helps with that." The doctor tapped the cane in his right hand against the floor. Zach was instantly drawn to the piece, which featured a noticeably detailed carved horse head with a sturdy, polished wood base.

"That's quite an eye-catcher. I've never seen another like it."

"You haven't?" Harry Rubin frowned. "That's surprising. Your father is the one who made it for me. A few years ago, right when my knees got worse and when he heard that my mare Crystal passed away, he showed up at my office with it." The doctor lifted the cane for Zach to get a closer look. "Crystal was like family to me, and your dad carved a spitting image of her. He'd trained her years ago, when you were a youngster. But I'm sure you were too busy being a young boy to know which horses were coming and going from your father's barn."

"*Jah*. Matthew and I cleaned those stalls and fed the horses, but sad to say, it was more of a chore than something special for us back then."

"Who can blame you?" Dr. Rubin laughed as he clasped Zach's shoulder. "We were all young once. Since you've been gone, maybe you also don't know about the carved horse heads on top of Robinson's brick driveway posts. Your dad sculpted those, too, for the same reason he carved this image of Crystal for me. Robinson's horses passed one after the other about three years ago. They were horses that your father also trained forever ago."

Zach's head spun, trying to take in everything the doctor was saying. How couldn't he have known these things about his own father? How were they such strangers? Before he could respond, Samuel was back beside him with his treasured treats, cookie crumbs dotting the sides of his mouth.

"Well, I'll let you two go so you can get home and enjoy more of those cookies." Dr. Rubin gently patted the top of Samuel's straw hat before looking up at Zach. "Tell your father hello for me, won't you? I hope he's recuperating well."

"He's getting there." At least, that was the truth physically, but with Samuel headed home, Zach had been wondering what would keep his father busy now.

"And tell him not to stop making these for people." Dr. Rubin tapped his cane on the wooden floor again. "It keeps the creatures God blessed our lives with close to us."

This time, Dr. Rubin extended his hand, and Zach was able to shake it. Afterward, he started to lead Samuel toward the bakery door when he suddenly stopped.

Was there a sign of *Gott* in the midst? Was the Lord trying to tell him something? Maybe the answer for his father?

He turned to see the doctor bent over the bakery counter, giving his order to Marianne. Zach stepped closer.

"Dr. Rubin, I hate to interrupt you, and I know this is asking a lot. But would you mind coming out to the farm and telling *Daed* yourself how much your cane means to you? I feel like it's something he could use hearing right now. Of course, if you could act like we never bumped into each other that would help too."

"How about tomorrow morning? I don't have office hours. Will that work?"

"That would be perfect. *Danke.* Thank you very much."

* * *

By the time Zach dropped Samuel off, Anna was so pleased to be home and to have all her children under one roof that she'd didn't argue with him about the cookies. At least not this time. She'd teased him as she thanked him for watching Samuel for the week and asked him to thank Leah and Ivan too.

All the way back to the farm, Zach was bursting with excitement. Kind of the same way Samuel had been in the bakery, he chuckled to himself. He couldn't wait to check on Leah. He couldn't wait to tell her what all he'd learned from the good doctor. He was eager to see what she thought about maybe, just maybe, when it came to his father's future, what the possibilities could be.

Leah had never been one to sit still. But hours after Thomas came to pick up Cat, she hadn't moved an inch from the sofa. Self-pity and disappointment had paralyzed her, turning her body and heart to stone.

When a knock repeatedly came at the front door, the heaviness kept her from going to answer it. Unfortunately, however, her cousin hadn't locked the door on her way out, allowing Zach to enter.

"Leah, are you here?"

She could hear the hopefulness in Zach's voice the moment he walked in. Yet the instant he stood before her, his face suddenly went grim. His brows drew together in an agonized expression. He crouched down, looking up at her uncertainly.

"Leah, what's going on? I know you're not *oll recht.*"

How a man who couldn't be trusted could appear so unbelievably concerned about her well-being was puzzling to her.

When she didn't answer right away, he attempted a smile. "I'm not sure what's going on with you, Leah. But I wish you'd tell me. Or even if you'd sigh for me, maybe that will tell me something I need to know."

"Zach," she responded dully. "Why are you here?"

He stiffened. "Because I want to be," he stammered. "Because I told you I'd check on you after you left the creek crying and leaving me worried ever since. And because I have some news that…well, something I wanted to share with you about my *daed.*"

"Oh, *now* you want to share?" she replied haughtily. "Well, Cat beat you to it. She told me all about your plan."

He stood up, his tall frame towering over her, his forehead furrowing even more. "I don't understand. I haven't even seen her. She wasn't at the bakery when I stopped by before taking Samuel home."

"She was there earlier, and Marianne told her everything."

"I'm... I'm lost, Leah." Shaking his head, he sank down onto the cushioned chair across from her. "I have no idea what you're talking about."

"Really? No idea about a deal with the Highland Property Development Company?"

His body froze instantly. He swallowed hard, looking as uncomfortable as she'd ever seen him.

"It's okay, Zach."

"No, Leah, it's not okay."

"It is now. I mean, at first, well, I was mighty angry with you. I couldn't believe you'd keep a secret from me. Or it's more like you lied to me, Zach."

He dipped his head repentantly, and why in her heart she believed he was sorry, she didn't know. But she did.

"But I see now that you're doing the right thing. You need to leave here and get on with your life. And if Highland buys your *daed*'s land, why, he can have a life too. A secure one where he doesn't have to worry about money. Sometimes we..." Sadness rankled through her, knowing she was thinking of herself as much as Ivan. "Sometimes we can't do much to control our destinies."

"Leah, this isn't like you. Your hopefulness is what has made a difference in me. And, *jah*, at first, I didn't tell you the truth. I mean the whole truth." He looked away as if he couldn't face her. "I was trying to keep you happy, saying we'd get *Daed* on his feet and the farm too. Which we did, didn't we? At the same time, I was hoping to find a way to lighten the load for Matthew, to free him up from responsibilities he doesn't have time for."

"You were seeking to be the man who can fix everything, huh?"

"I was. And in the beginning, I thought Highland was the answer. Which if you're solely looking at dollar amounts, it is. But I haven't given the proposal to *Daed* because somehow it doesn't feel totally right to me. The thing is, Leah, I think the Lord showed me something today. That's what I came to tell you. I think it's something that will work for my father. And for us too."

"For us?" Did he truly think they still had a future together? Like the future for them she'd been dreaming of and praying for? "No, Zach. There is no us. There can't be."

"But Leah…" His expression contorted sorrowfully. "There has to be."

"Well, there can't. Because if I'm being honest, I've been keeping a secret from you too."

Her admission left him wide-eyed. "About what?"

"I'm going blind, Zach."

She'd never said the word out loud. She'd only uttered it over and over in her head. But voicing it, hearing the sound of it, made reality hit harder.

Zach gaped at her, looking incredulous. But as soon as tears spilled from her eyes, he jumped out of his chair and was at her side. "Is that what all the crying was about at the creek?"

With tears trickling down her cheeks, she gazed at him and nodded.

"Oh, Leah." His voice was just as gentle as his touch as he reached out and drew her close. She let herself be coddled, needing a shoulder to finally cry on.

He rocked her in his arms soothingly, until she was ready to lift her head.

She pulled away from him, knowing she needed to distance herself. Zach didn't seem to be thinking the same way. He took her hand in his.

"Do you mind telling me what the diagnosis is? What doctor did you see?"

She sniffled and wiped her nose with her free hand. "I haven't seen a doctor. It's only gotten worse in the past few days. I'm sure it's the hereditary disease my aunt had."

"But you don't know that for sure."

"No, but what else could it be? I thought glasses would help with the wispy auras at the side of my eyes. I didn't even mention them to the optometrist, and he didn't pick up on them. But lately, they've gotten so much darker. And my vision… It's like I'm in a tunnel. Every day, it's harder to balance, harder to see. Until… I won't anymore." She shrugged, hopelessly. "I haven't told Cat because I don't want to ruin her wedding plans. I don't want her special time to turn into stuff about me. I just hope I can hang on that long." She choked back a sob. "Then I'll sell the house and find a nursing home I can afford and—"

"No, you're not doing any of that, Leah."

"I don't know another way."

"I do. I can take you to doctors anywhere in this country, anywhere in the world."

"Oh, I can't trust you, but now I'm going to trust a doctor? Like the one who misdiagnosed your *daed* and my little brother."

Obviously confused, Zach grimaced. "You never mentioned a little brother."

"Because it aches too much to speak of him. When Timmy fell on a pitchfork when he was five years old, the doctor didn't do right by him. That man sent my parents back home with medicine, saying the puncture wound would heal. Well, you know what?" She couldn't help her voice from rising. "The bacteria from the pitchfork got into my brother's bloodstream. He died, and everything inside my father died with him. My *daed* never forgave himself for trusting another man with his son's life."

"I can't begin to imagine how tragic that was."

"And that Christmas you and I talked about before? The one when our family came to Sugarcreek? It was the first Christmas after Timmy went to be with the Lord. I was skating on Stutzman's pond not ever wanting to stop because my mother was right here, in this house, crying her heart out to her mother—my *grossmammi*."

She bowed her head experiencing the sadness and devastation all over again. He lifted her chin with a gentle finger and gazed into her eyes.

"Leah, I want to help make things better.

I'll get you to the *verra* best doctors. We can do this, you'll see."

"That's just it, Zach. Like *Aenti* Naomi, I won't see. I've accepted that fact and you must too. You can't be bothered with this. You need to help your *daed* right now and do what's best for him."

"And what about what's best for you? For us?"

"You keep acting like there's an us, and I thought we shared something special too. I even let myself trust you. But, Zach, we've been lying to each other. What kind of relationship is that except for one without trust?"

"Was it really a lack of trust, Leah?" His eyes pleaded with her. "Maybe we were only trying to protect one another. Trying to get enough information before we shared what was on our minds."

"Who knows?" She lifted her hands in despair. "I only know that *Gott* always seems to put people in my life, and then He takes them away from me."

"You're wrong." His tone turned gruff. "The Lord isn't taking them away, Leah. You're doing that yourself. Have you ever thought that maybe He's brought people into your life to help you? Do you think you're the only caregiver *Gott* ever put on this earth?"

Her lips began to tremble, hearing the honesty and the frustration in his voice.

"Look, I don't want to make you cry again. But you've got to know that I don't want you to give up. I don't want to lose you or not be there for you. My father would say the same thing. Your cousin would, too, along with Matthew and Anna, your students and everyone else who knows you. Don't forget, *Gott* placed you into all our lives and that means something. You mean a lot to me, Leah."

She might've been losing her eyesight, but that didn't stop her from seeing the earnestness in Zach's expression or from feeling that everything he said was the purest truth. Still, she didn't want to be a burden. How was that fair to anyone?

"Zach, I'm tired. Really tired. Do you mind leaving now, please?" She rose from the couch.

He sighed and shook his head, visibly distressed. "*Jah*, I'll go, and you can shut me out all you want. But you'll never stop me from caring about you, Leah. Not ever."

Hours later, Leah glanced out her kitchen window at the house next door. With a yearning sadness, she realized the home she'd been such a part of appeared so distant now—as if it was a hundred miles away. And that feeling had nothing to do with her diminishing vision.

Rather, it was because inside that house was Zach, the man who wanted everything for her. The man who had stolen her heart. And she'd pushed him away.

Suddenly, knocking sounded and her pulse quickened. If it was Zach again, what would she do? What should she say? Cautiously making her way to the door, she opened it and was stunned. There stood Charlotte.

"Hi, Miss Leah." Her young student gave a timid wave while her mother Pamela stood at the bottom of the steps, smiling.

"Charlotte. Pamela. What a nice surprise. Would you like to come in?"

"Oh, no, we can't stay." Pamela waved a hand. "We're leaving for vacation tomorrow, heading to the Outer Banks. But since Charlotte won't be here for your last summer tutoring session next week, she wanted to stop by."

Her tutoring session! She'd been stewing about it, wondering how she was going to handle that. Could she even make it into town on her own?

"I have a present for you, Miss Leah," Charlotte spoke up.

"You do?"

"It's this." The sweet child hadn't appeared very shy before, yet she did now as she presented Leah with a booklet bound by blue yarn. "It's a book I made called '*If You Hear a Bird Tweet*.'"

"Oh, Charlotte." Taking the book into her hands, Leah was overwhelmed. "I don't have my glasses right now, but I can't wait to read it."

"It's not too long. I know it by heart. It says, 'If you hear a bird tweet it sounds sweet. That makes you want sugar to eat. So you go to the bakery down the street. You get a treat. Isn't that neat?'"

Leah laughed delightedly. "I love it," she exclaimed, causing a huge grin to spread across the child's face.

"Mom helped with some of the handwriting and spelling. But the words are mine and so are the pictures. I'm the author and the—" She turned to seek her mother's help.

"Illustrator," Pamela interjected. "Miss Leah, you're the mentor who helped her enjoy reading more which led to her doing this."

"I—I don't know what to say." She hugged the book to her chest. "This book is priceless to me, Charlotte. It always will be. Thank you for creating it."

"You'll let us know when your sessions start up again in the fall, won't you?" Pamela asked.

"I, uh…" Leah swallowed hard. Before she could answer, Pamela had more to say.

"We'll find time to be there, and I'm sure the other kids and moms will too. We see them all a lot now since we're scheduling trips to the library together."

Again, Leah was moved nearly beyond words. "That's wonderful."

"Well, we best get going. I still have packing to do. You ready, Charlotte?"

"Oh, wait!" Somehow, Leah didn't feel right not giving anything to Charlotte in return. Hurrying to her bedroom, nearly tripping over everything in her path, she wasn't sure what that could be. But then it came to her. Gathering up craft paper, markers, stickers and ribbon, she placed the items in a small tote and headed back to the front door.

"Here's a little something in case you want to make another book. Maybe one about your vacation and a grabby crab or something?"

Charlotte took the satchel, her smile wide as she glanced inside it.

"What do you say, Charlotte?" her mother prompted.

"Thank you. Thanks a lot!"

"No, thank you, Charlotte. You have a wonderful vacation and safe travels."

Leah waved as mother and daughter drove away. As she did, a warm rush of emotion welled up in her again. But this time instead of drowning in fear and sorrow, she was overcome with gratitude and hope.

"Oh, Lord, you are watching over me, ain't so? I promise to do everything I can in Your Name to get my eyes well, starting tomorrow."

Glancing over at the Graber house again, she knew what the first item of healing needed to be. That was to mend the relationship with the caring man next door.

Chapter Fourteen

The next morning Zach and his father sat at the kitchen table with a plateful of Danish between them, and sunlight pouring in the window all around them. When they suddenly heard a knock at the door, his father's brows creased curiously.

"Who could that be so early? It couldn't be Leah, could it? Why would she be knocking?"

"Doubtful, *Daed*. She hasn't been working on Saturdays."

But, of course, that wasn't the only reason Zach suspected it wasn't her. After the way their conversation had ended the day before, he wondered when they'd ever speak again. It was a question that had kept him awake all night. Especially knowing how she was suffering and how much he longed to be there for her.

Besides, he had a plenty good idea who the

visitor might be. Still, he pretended otherwise and popped up out of his chair. "I'll see who it is."

As soon as he opened the door, Zach felt a strange twinge of relief at the sight of Dr. Rubin. It was partly because the man's visit posed a brief distraction from his concerns for Leah. But he was also hopeful of what a talk with the doctor might prod his father to do. At once Dr. Rubin gave Zach a conspiratorial sort of wink and smile—like a well-meaning accessory to a good cause—that had Zach grinning too.

"Zach! It's great to see you. You're looking well," the doctor exclaimed as if he hadn't seen Zach just the day before. Obviously, the doctor was intent on playing his role well and being plenty loud enough that his father could hear.

"Same to you." Zach held out his hand and the two of them shook. "Are you out making house calls this morning?" he asked, feeling like he was reciting lines from a skit.

"Ah, no. I was just passing by and thought I'd drop in to say hello to your father."

"*Willkumme.* Come on in."

Zach led Dr. Rubin into the kitchen and wasn't sure how his *daed* would react to having the good doctor drop in even before he'd finished his morning coffee. But Zach needn't have worried. His father looked pleased by the seemingly impromptu visit from a friend.

"Dr. Harry, how are you?" His father started to get up. "Can I get you a plate for a Danish? We have plenty."

"No, no. I'm good." Dr. Rubin motioned for Zach's father to sit. "Millie filled me up before I headed out to run errands this morning."

"Have a seat then," his father offered. "And, Zach, get the good doctor some coffee. Or would you rather have juice?"

"No, coffee is fine. Just black," Dr. Rubin told Zach as he settled into a chair.

For once, Zach didn't mind taking orders from his father. After setting a cup of steaming coffee in front of Dr. Rubin, he busied himself doing dishes and puttering around the kitchen. Far enough away not to be involved in the men's conversation, but close enough to overhear it.

"So, how are you doing, Ivan?" Dr. Rubin asked. "Getting better, I hope?"

"*Jah*, just not as quickly as I'd expected. But then I hear these kinds of injuries take time."

"Absolutely. You took quite a spill."

"It was nasty, for sure, especially at this age. And honestly, Doc…" Zach noticed how his father leaned over the table, speaking candidly, "I don't know what to think anymore."

"Do you mean about work? Or possibly retirement?"

"I don't see how I can afford to retire. And I'd be bored stiff, like I already am right now." He paused. "I do know they say if you fall off a horse to get back on it. But…"

Zach heard the doctor reply, "Yes, it's tough at this age. Why, with my knee after my car accident, I've never been the same either. At work I had to cut back hours and let my younger partner take on some of the weightier issues and heftier patients."

Zach's father laughed at that. "I have a few people in mind that you may be thinking of, but the Lord may not like me saying their names out loud."

Zach tried to recall a time when he'd witnessed his father in a conversation with a friend. For sure, this was a different side of him than Zach had ever seen.

"I agree with you, though, Ivan. This time of life isn't bad, but I believe it does take some readjusting and any assistance we can get. Like this keepsake you made me." Zach noticed Dr. Rubin stop and tighten his grip on the cane his father had created. "I use this all the time."

"Crystal was a good one," his father replied solemnly.

"That she was. And you did a fantastic job

of preserving her memory for me. Which had me and Millie thinking. Her brother's mare of twenty-four years just passed, and you know how hard that is."

"It's difficult for sure."

"She wanted me to ask if you'd do a small carving for him."

"But I don't know the horse."

"That's not a problem if you're up to the task. Millie has pictures of the horse on her phone that she can print for you. Of course, if I thought you were right-handed, after your sprain, I wouldn't even be asking. But I know that's not the case."

"This doctor friend of mine has a great memory," his *daed* commented, turning to include Zach.

"It comes with the territory," Dr. Rubin replied, giving Zach a smile. Then taking a last sip of coffee, he got up out of the chair. With his cane in front of him, he hugged the carving with both hands, one on top of the other. "What do you say, Ivan? Can I at least tell Millie you're thinking about doing the sculpting?"

Zach heard his father sigh, but even as he did, a slightly satisfied-looking smile twitched at the corners of his mouth. "Ah, if it's for Millie, just go ahead and tell her yes."

Gaping at his father, Zach blinked in disbelief. Had he really heard his obstinate father give in so easily? Could the hopes he had for him be coming to fruition so handily?

"You're turning out to be a real softy in your old age," Dr. Rubin commented.

Ivan reached down and patted his own flabby belly. "I'd say we both are, my friend."

The men shared a good laugh and a warm clasp of hands before Zach escorted the doctor out the door and onto the porch. He was barely able to contain himself, bursting with gratitude. But he willed himself to be discreet, not going overboard or taking a risk of being overheard. Why take a chance on what he thought could be his father's future—and what he hoped might create a different kind of future for himself too?

Looking back, Leah thought it might've been silly of her. But while the stark reality of losing her eyesight had left her emotionally drained and physically weak the day before, she had made sure to awaken early. Her goal was to take her time getting dressed, wishing to look her best before heading over to Ivan's house to ask for Zach's forgiveness.

Ultimately, Zach had been right about what he'd said, and she shouldn't have argued with him. They'd both been keeping secrets from each other, hoping not to worry the other. Zach had also been correct in insisting she see a doctor. And to that end, she also wanted to appear ready and willing to seek the professional help she believed *Gott* had shown her she so desperately needed. Like her grandmother used to say, why ask the Lord to guide your footsteps if you're not willing to move your feet?

With all that in mind, she'd combed through her hair several times, carefully tying her reddish-brown locks into a bun. Then she added a freshly washed *kapp* that her grandmother had stitched shortly before she passed. She'd even applied a smidgen of lip balm. Thankfully, her emerald dress was waiting for her in the closet. The same dress that Cat had told her time and again highlighted her hazel green eyes so perfectly.

And, oh, how her eyes needed a touch of brightness.

Even as brilliant as the morning sunshine was as she crossed the lawns to the Graber house, her diminished vision eclipsed the light, leaving her surroundings shadowed in darkness. Yet, thankfully, she could still see enough to make out Zach's brawny build on the porch steps. She also recognized Dr. Rubin with his white tufts of hair and his cane, always close at hand.

At first, glimpsing the doctor concerned her—she wondered if something might be wrong with Ivan. But the closer she got, her worry subsided. Both men sounded far too jovial for that to be the case. Facing each other, so engrossed were they in their chatting, they didn't even notice her approach. Rather than interrupt them, she halted her steps and thought about going back home.

And she would've. Except for one thing. There was something about the pleased tone in Zach's voice that heightened her curiosity. Which meant she couldn't tear herself away. Instead, she slipped in next to a towering oakleaf hydrangea brimming with full white blooms at the side of the house. Unwittingly, her green dress and white *kapp* had turned out to be the best camouflage ever. Tilting her head, she leaned in to listen.

"Dr. Rubin, you're not only a great physician but the Lord has blessed you with a gift to heal a person's spirit too," Zach was saying.

"The Lord does provide healing in many ways, doesn't He? If we're open to it, that is."

"For sure. I can't tell you how much I appreciate you dropping by. Oh, and I do have one other question for you. Who would you recommend as the best ophthalmologist in town?"

"Is your father having eye issues?"

Leah froze, hoping Zach wouldn't reveal her name. Somehow it didn't feel right for anyone to know about her issue until she took steps to confide in her cousin and Ivan.

"*Nee*, it's for a friend."

A sigh of relief erupted from her. She covered her mouth instantly as if that could cancel out the sound that had already escaped her. Peeking up at the porch, she saw the men were still talking and oblivious to her hovering nearby.

On one hand, Zach was as sweet as could be and she was touched that he'd attempted to find help for her. But on the other hand? Why did it always feel like he was trying to go around her? Not just with her issues but with everything. Sometimes it was exasperating that he was such a fixer.

But then what about me? Could Zach be just as tired of me trying to do everything on my own?

She pondered the question until Dr. Rubin replied.

"Dr. Samantha Cooper would be at the top of my list."

"Okay, *danke*. I'll pass that along."

"Zach, it sounds like your father and friend are fortunate to have you here right now. But your home is in Shipshewana, right?"

"My house is in Indiana, *jah*."

"Well, if I don't see you before you head back, it's been a pleasure."

"For me as well, Dr. Rubin. Let me walk you to your car."

While the men headed down the steps and toward the driveway, they appeared to still be reveling in something. It was nothing she had any idea about, but whatever it was seemed to be positive and promising.

More than anything, she wished she could feel the same way. But how could she when the reminder of Zach's imminent departure for Indiana weighed so devastatingly heavy on her?

Whereas Zach's shoulders were square and broad, appearing strong enough to take on the world, hers slumped resignedly with her arms dangling at her sides. And while the lighthearted grin on his face was one that usually made her smile, too, in contrast her heart ached in a way that was becoming quite familiar to her.

She was losing her eyesight. But how could she have possibly lost sight of the fact that Zach wasn't meant to remain in Sugarcreek? That he wasn't there to stay?

Yes, she'd said the same thing over and over, warning herself. Yet regrettably, in the deepest part of her, she had never chosen to believe it, had she? How could she when her heart hadn't wanted to?

Rather, she'd placed too much importance on their near kiss. She'd put too much hope in their hands clasped together in the sunshine. And had poured so much faith and trust into his warm words of admiration and his tender looks of affection.

For sure and certain, there had been a sharing between them like she'd never known before. But how naive of her to think it was all more than a gesture. None of it meant a lifetime of happily-ever-after. None of it was permanent. Not any of it. No matter how much she may have wanted it to be.

Just because Zach was a kind man who said he wanted to help—that didn't mean anything lasting. The reality was, besides her, he had plenty to do to get Ivan settled. And ultimately, a life awaiting him a state away.

Tears welled up in her eyes at the truth of that and began slipping down her cheeks. With every part of her being, she was determined to brush each drop away.

She would seek out doctors. She would stay strong. More than that, she would trust that *Gott* would accompany her along whatever path He laid before her.

Chapter Fifteen

After saying his goodbyes to Dr. Rubin and thanking him again, Zach ran up the steps and into the house, feeling hopeful. That sensation didn't last long, however, when he saw his father in the sitting room, his arms crossed over his chest.

"You were always the clever one in the family. Or trying to be, anyway."

Zach's body stiffened at his father's curt tone, not sure what had changed his humor in the last few minutes. "I'm not sure what you mean," he replied, his optimism quickly fading.

"I don't think it's an accident that Doc happened to stop by just now."

"How so?"

"Well, I'm no detective, but you brought home cookies from Sunshine Bakery yesterday. Doc is often there since he's a partner with the owners and—"

"He is?"

His father gave a wry smile. "I'm guessing you saw him there?"

Zach nodded. "No one meant to lie to you, *Daed*."

"I know. You're just trying to look out for me. Trying to help me find my way. Which is remarkable after what I did to you five years ago. Or at least, what I'm sure you *thought* I did."

Those words from his father slammed into him, leaving him shaking down to his legs. Feeling unstable, he collapsed into the nearest chair, finding it hard to conceive that the moment he'd hoped for had finally come. It was time for them to get the past out into the open.

Yet seeing the deep lines on his father's face, knowing all that his *daed* had been through—and not knowing what lay ahead—somehow a part of him wished to grant the man who'd sired him grace.

And if he did, would there be any way possible for him to receive the same kind of judgment?

"It was a long time ago, *Daed*."

"It's not when you carry it around with you each day."

At first, Zach didn't think he'd heard right. But as the words sunk in, he realized he had.

All the years of hurt and grief and wondering, accumulated inside him, becoming staggering. He gripped the arms of the chair and swallowed with difficulty, fighting to control his emotions.

"You too?" he asked hoarsely.

His father nodded solemnly.

"I… I don't understand. Then why? Why didn't you answer my letters?"

"It's a long story and not one I've ever told."

While his father stared hard at him, Zach was unsure how to respond. Except to sit still, ready to listen in case his *daed* decided to share.

It was minutes before his father spoke another word.

"It's not easy knowing where to start. Some things you don't want to talk about, especially in detail. Not that I'm a fluffy kind of man anyway."

Zach smiled wanly at that. "Mighty true."

"*Jah*, you know that about me. But what you don't know is that I'm not the person you or Matthew think I am."

Another bolt of shock surged through Zach. "What do you mean?"

"Well, for starters, I was born to *Englisch* parents."

"You're—not Amish?" The flood of astonishment kept coming, knocking Zach deeper into his seat.

"Of course, I am. But like I said, I wasn't born that way. I never knew my father, and my mother was a drug addict. She wasn't around too often when she was alive. I was pretty much orphaned and had to survive on my own. It was not a good start to life."

The admission came so fast, Zach could barely take it all in. He was trying to process what he'd heard as his father continued.

"And don't go looking at me all wide-eyed, not knowing what to say—because there is nothing for you to say. I'll have you know, thanks be to *Gott*, life did get better for me after a while. Only because I met your mother when we were around ten years old."

"It sounds like an incredible blessing that you survived that long on your own."

"Oh, it was. I did odd jobs around town when I could find them and then went stealing when I couldn't. One day not too long after my mother died, I was having hunger pains. So I went to steal some peanut butter crackers at the drugstore. I got caught, and you know what?" His father's mouth crinkled into a wistful smile that was even more puzzling.

"I can't even imagine." Zach shook his head.

"It was the best thing that ever happened to

me. Because suddenly there was a girl standing next to me. She had the prettiest blue eyes I'd ever seen and some curly blond hair coming out of the top of her *kapp*." His father grinned, remembering. "And while I was shaking in my holey shoes, she made up a story, telling the store manager that my pocketing the crackers was all a misunderstanding and a game we were playing. Then she bought those crackers for me using money she'd earned helping an elderly neighbor."

"That was *Mamm*?"

"Oh, *jah*." His father chuckled. "That was your mother."

"It sounds like her, for sure, always wanting to help others."

"And that's not all. She brought me to her house and her parents didn't take me in, but they found a home for me with their Amish neighbors. They were an elderly couple who were childless. They didn't exactly treat me like their child. Never sent me to school, but then my own mother hadn't either." His father's voice quieted some. "I'd get jealous some mornings watching the Amish kids go by on their way to the schoolhouse. By then, I'd already been out in the fields for hours or taking care of the horses."

His father stopped, releasing a sigh. "All the

same, the couple did feed me and put some fat on my bones. They provided a roof over my head and a warm bed for me to sleep in. Although they didn't officially adopt me, they did give me their family name of Graber since I had no family to speak of. And Benjamin Graber taught me all I know about training horses."

"I... I don't know what to say."

"I already told you—there's nothing for you to say. When the Graber couple passed, surprisingly they left me with another blessing— their land. Once your mother and I married, I sold it and we moved from Wayne County to here in Tuscarawas County. And the reason I'm telling you all of this, Zach, isn't for you to feel sorry for me. It's for me to say that I'm sorry to you. Pure and simple, I didn't grow up being loved by parents. The Grabers were kind but standoffish. Guess I've never known how to show love. So I veered all my attention and affection to what I knew best—horses."

It occurred to Zach then why even on her deathbed, his mother had never complained that his father wasn't near. "But knowing you since you both were *kinner*, *Mamm* sensed your love."

"She also did my reading for me since I never had any schooling. I can barely read enough to get by and was always too embarrassed for anyone to know that except for your *mamm*. That's why I was unable to read or answer your letters, Zach. They're still unopened in a box in my closet." He paused before going on. "When you left for Indiana, it crushed me. But deep down, I figured it was for the best. You always had a good brain, the smartest one in our family, and you could figure out how to fix anything."

"I wish you would've told me back then."

"I wish I would've too. I think we were both hurting plenty when your mother went to be with the Lord. I really thought you'd be better off not being around someone in your life who couldn't show they cared or loved you like your mother had. And now, looking back, I realize how wrong I was. I don't blame you for not thinking much of me."

"Honestly, *Daed*, what I'm thinking right now is that I'm thankful. Having you share like this is all I've ever wanted. But I didn't know if we'd ever get to this point. When I first got here, you didn't give me much of a welcome."

"*Jah*, it was my confusing way of caring, thinking you'd be better off getting back to your life. But you've stuck around."

"And I'm glad I did. It's been healing for me. All my life I thought you cared more about your horses than me. And I thought you'd never forgive me for the accident. I never meant to hurt Amos." Zach's voice cracked, uttering the horse's name. "I hope you believe me."

"I do. You're too good of a man for that, Zach."

"You don't know how much it means for me to hear you say that, *Daed*." He began welling up. "I don't want either of us to hurt anymore."

"I don't either." His father's eyes turned misty.

Zach couldn't remember a time when he'd reached out and hugged his father, but he couldn't help himself. And it felt like a weight was lifted from his shoulders and his world, when his father hugged him in return. An indescribable peace filled him as he realized how *Gott* had managed to give them this time together.

As a teenager, he'd cursed the day that the Lord had taken his perfect parent from him. He'd yelled at the Creator for removing the only loving person from his life. Of course, *Gott* knew all along that it was far better to take his mother instead of the father he struggled with. The Lord also knew there'd come a time when, if willing, he and his father could set things right with each other.

After clasping shoulders, there was a short

silence, along with grateful glimpses at one another. And then, father like son, they both glanced away as they swiped at their eyes.

Feeling so appreciative that he might at last have a real relationship with his father after this redemption from the past, Zach almost hated to bring up the present. But he had to.

"As long as we're being honest here, *Daed*, there's something I need to talk to you about too. And I also don't know where to start…" His voice drifted.

His father held up a hand. "I think I know what you're going to say. I've let Leah believe I could keep on training horses and continue managing this property. For a while, I believed the same thing. But I'm glad you did have Doc drop by because talking with him was good for me. At this age, life does change. I don't think this body of mine is up to training horses anymore."

After decades of his father's dedication to his profession, the importance of his father's acknowledgment seemed to reverberate throughout the room.

"I know that has to be hard for you to say out loud."

"It is," his father agreed. Even so, his eyes twinkled just slightly. "But it seems I've been saying a lot of things out loud just now that

I never thought I would say. And in a way, it feels good."

Zach chuckled. "I know what you mean." He paused then, praying that he could say the rest of what needed to be said tactfully, and without getting a rise from his father. "I'm glad you're not considering horse training in the future because I've been researching two options for you. If you're willing to listen."

"You know more about what's going on beyond this farm than I do."

"Well, to put it bluntly, the Highland Property Development Company is ready to purchase your farm for a substantial sum of money. More than enough money that would provide a financially secure future for you if managed properly."

His father frowned. "Why would they do that?"

"So they can build a condominium complex."

"A what?"

"You heard right."

"And the other option?"

"You can start a new business and have a new sense of purpose."

"Let me guess. You mean wood carving?"

"I know mother's friend Frieda Stoltz is

looking for someone to share her Amish gift-ware shop in town."

"And you think that could make a living for me?" His father eyed him as if he was *verrickt*, crazy.

"No, I don't," he answered frankly.

"Oh, I think I understand. The rumor I heard is true then? Are you really a wealthy man and you're going to pay for a place for me to live in?"

Taken aback, Zach's heart began to race. "Who did you hear that from?"

"Does it matter?"

For years, he'd been working hard to keep the success the Lord had blessed him with as a secret. It had been more important to him to use that wealth to discreetly help others. But since his father had been so open with him, how could he not do the same?

"If I tell you the truth, can you keep a secret?"

"I'd say I've spent my adult life keeping one about myself." His father grinned.

"Yes, then, I'm telling you *Gott* has blessed me with an abundance of wealth as a silent investor in various Amish businesses in several states."

"So, are you thinking you'd be a silent investor in my property? I'm not sure I understand."

"Well... I..." He bit his lip, wanting to explain, but also hoping not to be rejected. "*Daed*, when Leah reached out to me, I was glad to come back to help. But I admit, I didn't come for you as much as for myself. I wanted the chance to seek redemption from you... Forgiveness. But the longer I've been back home, the more I want a future here, just as much as you do. I love it here, *Daed*. I enjoy being around family and the horses. Now I understand what you've always seen in those amazing creatures. Oddly, I even like being in this house with its strange accumulation of memories."

He took a deep breath before daring to continue. "*Daed*, I don't want to go back to Indiana. I'd *verra* much like to live here with you. And also, hopefully in the very near future, with a wife and *kinner*."

"Whoa." His father held up a hand. "I love my *grosskinner*. But I'm too old to live with all that racket. I think I'd want my own place."

"Fine. There's plenty of room on this property. I can build a *dawdi haus* for you."

"I could live with that but only if I pay some sort of rent."

"I'm sure we can work out something to suit you."

"There's only one thing I don't understand.

When you're talking about a *frau*, would that be Leah you're thinking of?"

"*Jah*, it is. I've never loved like this before. But it could all be just a dream that I need to wake up from. She's not happy with me right now." He didn't feel right about explaining all the reasons why.

"You're a smart man, son. You can figure out a way to change that."

"I suppose you're right." He leaned back in the chair, folding his arms over his chest and silently praying that his father was indeed correct.

"Then again, maybe you're not as smart as I think you are," his father clucked.

"What do you mean?"

"I can't believe you're still sitting here. It's a new day the Lord has made, Zach. You need to get next door."

Even though Leah hadn't made the effort in the past half hour to look at the Bible opened to Psalms in her lap, it still felt comforting to have *Gott*'s Word near. The sudden burst of rain pitter-pattering on the rooftop soothed as well. The summer shower meant she couldn't hang laundry, mow the lawn, weed the garden or do any other outdoor job that would be difficult with her loss of vision. She closed her eyes and listened to the raindrops, whispering her thanks in the silence of her house. Then she startled at the rapping on her door.

Closing the Bible, she set it on a side table and wobbled her way to the entrance. Although she couldn't imagine who it would be except for Zach, she had been surprised earlier. But when she opened the door, this time she was right.

Zach was standing there, rain dripping from his clothes, concern in his eyes. Right away, she thought perhaps she'd misjudged the reason for Dr. Rubin's visit that she'd witnessed earlier.

"Zach, come in."

As he stepped inside and removed his wet straw hat, she was acutely aware of how the tall, handsome man instantly filled her living space. Not to mention her heart. Even so, pushing those feelings aside, she turned her thoughts to his father. "Is Ivan *oll recht*?"

"He is. More than fine. But I need to talk to you, Leah." His eyes pleaded.

"Sure."

He blinked in complete surprise when she answered so willingly. A twinge of regret jabbed at her for causing the strain between them as she held out her hand for his hat. After taking it though, hard as she tried, she couldn't manage to hang it on a hook by her door. Noticing, he covered his warm hand over hers to assist her. All at once, the recollection of another time of closeness caused her cheeks to flush beyond her control. She attempted to ignore the sensation as they made their way to the sofa where she began to ask questions.

"You say Ivan is fine?"

"He is. And I'm better now too. And it's all because of you, *danke*."

She eyed him quizzically.

"If you hadn't reached out to me, *Daed* and I would've never had the conversation we had just now. We may never have had the chance to forgive one another—or even get to know each other better."

"Zach, that's so wonderful. I know you've been waiting so long for that. But it's not because of me that happened. I asked, and you came. The circumstances led you here, and I'm guessing *Gott* knew both your hearts were ready to heal."

"And what about you, Leah? Like I said before, don't you think it's the same for you and what you're going through? I'm sorry for how I messed up before, but you can trust that I want to help you."

She lowered her head, not wanting to look at him and call to mind everything about him that she couldn't see as well as she once had. Like his cropped light brown hair that he ran his fingers through when he was perplexed or feeling shy. His square jawline that mirrored his quiet, God-given strength. And the sincerity in his bluer-than-blue eyes that was so mighty hard to resist. Like now.

"I know you want to help, Zach," she murmured. "But you're not responsible for me."

He lifted her chin to meet his gaze. "What if I want to be?"

"Oh, Zach." She groaned, resisting the temptation to lean closer to him. Ever so gently, she removed his hand. "I appreciate your kindness, I do. But I don't want to be a bother to you."

"Oh, but you're already a bother to me, Leah Zook."

"I am?"

"*Jah*, you are. In fact, you bother me day and night." His voice raised.

"I do?" she replied meekly, caught completely off guard. "You never said so before."

"Well, it's true. I get bothered by you all the time. Like when I can't stop thinking about you. And when I can't wait to see you to tell you what's been happening in my day. And then that smile of yours…"

She touched her lips self-consciously. "What's wrong with my smile?"

"Nothing." He shook his head. "Nothing at all. Except it makes me want to do anything you ask of me and everything you don't ask."

"Oh… Now I'm understanding. I'm thinking you mean like taking me to see a doctor."

"*Jah*, like that. And if you won't go to the doctor for yourself, then I'm telling you, you need to go for Ivan."

"I'm confused, Zach. You said Ivan is fine."

"He is. But he can't read, Leah, not much anyway."

"Oh, I should've known!" She sat up straight. "It's not like that thought never crossed my mind. Sometimes he'd have me read stories to him. And other times he'd squint like he couldn't see well enough to read something, and he'd pass it on to me. But when it came to him spotting any teeny-weeny stain on his shirt I couldn't get washed out, oh, his eyes were plenty good enough then." She chuckled lightheartedly.

"And by going to a doctor and getting fixed up, well, then you'll be able to tutor the man." Zach's brows raised expectantly. "I know you'd love to."

"You don't have to twist my arm. The Lord has already done that. One of my students stopped by last night, and…" Recalling Charlotte's visit and the Lord's timing, her heart swelled. "I've already decided to see a doctor, Zach."

"I've heard Dr. Samantha Cooper is a good choice. I'll call on Monday for you, and I'm taking you there too."

"Zach, I've got to do this myself. You need to concentrate on your *daed*, and then you have a home in Indiana that you need to get back to."

"Who says I do?"

"Well, you did. Even just this morning you said so."

Justifiably, he appeared confused. "But we never spoke this morning."

"You're right. We didn't, but you and Dr. Rubin did. I heard you when I was hiding by the porch near the hydrangea."

She wasn't sure what his reaction to her admission would be. She was thankful when he seemed amused.

"You were hiding?" He crooked a smile. "Why?"

"I came over to apologize for being rude to you yesterday." Her cheeks flushed as she explained. "You were only trying to be kind to me, and I'm sorry. *Verra* sorry."

"I'd say we both have something to be sorry about, Leah. But I hope we're past that now?"

"I do too. I really do." She sighed. "I also hope you can forgive me for eavesdropping.

But when I heard you and Dr. Rubin talking, I couldn't help myself. And when he asked if your home was still in Shipshewana, you answered yes."

"You heard wrong, Leah."

"No, I really don't think I did," she countered.

"What I said is that I have a house in Indiana. I never mentioned a home there. And after speaking with *Daed*, that's another thing I wanted to talk to you about." He paused, earnestly studying her face. "I don't want to leave Sugarcreek or even Graber Horse Farm, Leah. And I especially don't want to if you'll give me a reason to stay."

"Oh, Zach, you're so good to me." Tears filled her eyes. "Too good to me. But first things first. You can't make a commitment like that not knowing what's going to happen with me and my vision."

His lips curved slightly as he gazed at her lovingly, reassuringly. "*Jah*, I can, Leah. I'm ready to. The question is, can you?"

Chapter Sixteen

On the morning of her Tuesday appointment with Dr. Cooper, Leah shouldn't have been surprised to find her sweet cousin sitting at the kitchen table with a mug of coffee and a scone waiting for her. But even so, she was caught off guard. Beyond that, she was also touched.

"Shouldn't you be at work, Cat?" She took careful steps across the kitchen, settling in across from the thoughtful *maedel*, welcoming the freshly brewed drink in her hands.

"Marianne owed me a favor. I've covered for her plenty when the poor girl was out with morning sickness."

"But Zach will be here shortly with the driver to pick me up."

"Yes, he will. And until then, I wanted to stay close by."

"You know what?" Leah reached across

the table and squeezed Cat's hand. "I'm glad. *Danke.* At least being here with you my brain may stop reeling a million miles a minute. I seem to go from one worry to the next. Then, I say two prayers to cancel out the worry before the cycle starts all over again."

"I hope with all that thinking that you're including happy thoughts of Zach, cousin."

"Oh, Cat. He's in my thoughts. He's in my heart. He's everywhere when he's not even near. And it's got to stop. I can't do this to him."

"Do what? Be the woman he loves and the woman who loves him?"

"But I don't want to complicate his life, Cat. It's not fair to him."

"And yet he wants to be there for you, Leah."

"Oh." Leah waved a hand. "Of course, he would. That's his nature. He sees a problem and wants to make it right."

"I don't know, cousin. I think with you he sees something right and wants to hold on to it."

Leah's lips quivered, knowing how true Cat's words were—even for herself. "And I want to hold on too. I love him like I've never loved anyone before. But like he's ready to give everything for me, I want to do the same for him. And just because I'm faced with the fear of going blind, what kind of caring person would I be—what kind of a true love would I be—if I didn't care and love him enough to let him go?"

The question seemed to echo in the silence that hung between them. A minute passed before Cat dipped her head, apologetically. "I'm sorry, Leah. I shouldn't have pushed. Instead I should simply be praying."

"Cat, don't be sorry. I know you only want the best for me."

"We Zook girls are the same that way, ain't so?"

Leah smiled. "That we are. And even when you're a Lehman we will be."

"Definitely." It was Cat's turn to pat Leah's hand.

"It's silly of me, I know, but…" Leah started, then bit her tongue.

"But what?"

"Oh, nothing." Leah shook her head.

"You have to tell me. Otherwise, I'll be imagining all kinds of things if you don't."

"Well, I keep wondering if *Aenti* Naomi Zook was in love before she went blind."

Cat frowned. "Why would you wonder that?"

"I suppose only because if I have the same hereditary eye disease that she had, well, then

I can truly feel what she went through. But who's to know? My parents never talked about her. With us living in West Union, maybe she wasn't at the top of their minds. They were both such caring people though, so it's strange I never heard of her."

Cat choked on a sip of coffee before slowly setting her mug on the tabletop. "Leah, I don't know how to tell you this because I don't know if it's comforting or not. But *Aenti* Naomi was not related to either of us in any way."

"But you said—"

"*Jah*, I did and I'm sorry I didn't explain. Please forgive me. Have you been thinking all along that you have the same disease as she had?"

"Why wouldn't I?"

"I should've told you that Naomi Zook wasn't a part of our family. She was a friend of my mother who lived down the street from *Mamm* when she was growing up. And since she had the same last name as we did, we used to refer to her as our *Aenti* Naomi Zook. When her blindness set in due to *her* family's hereditary issues, *Mamm* and *Daed* would take cookies and treats to her at the nursing facility where she lived until she passed."

"So, I—" Disbelieving, Leah shook her

head. "So, there's no chance I have a hereditary disease?"

"Not any chance that I'm aware of."

Leah let go of a sigh, instantly feeling relieved. Until her head began spinning again.
And tremors of alarm coursed through every
part of her body. What was causing her loss
of vision then? Something worse? Something
just as awful?

Oh, dearest Lord, please help me!

She kept repeating her plea to Heaven as she
shakily raised the mug to her lips. She managed to take a sip without sloshing a drop, and
for her dear cousin's sake, did everything she
could to appear calm. Even though her mind
was reeling again, totally out of control.

The ophthalmologist's office was on the far
outskirts of town. Making the trip by buggy
would've been unthinkable and unsafe. By car,
Zach knew it would take nearly a half hour. Yet
sitting next to Leah in the back seat of an *Englisch* driver's SUV, he could tell the ride probably felt like it was taking forever to her. He
got the impression she was holding her breath
as she rubbed at her hands, appearing too nervous at times to even glance at him.

At first, he attempted to make small talk,
trying to distract her and make the time go by

more quickly. But when she barely responded, he reached out and held her hand in the most reassuring way that he could. It was then that she looked over at him. And even though her vision wasn't what it should be, undoubtedly there was a look of appreciation in her eyes that he could see. Encouraged by that, he clasped her hand gently, lovingly, during the entire drive.

It wasn't until they reached their destination and the driver pulled into the office building parking lot, that Leah finally spoke.

"We're here?" she rasped.

"We are."

"Oh, Zach, I'm so scared." The anxious look on her blanched face made him want to envelop her protectively into his arms. So he did, too hopelessly beside himself to care that the driver might see.

"Everything's going to be *oll recht*," he whispered. "I'm here for you no matter what. And never forget, *Gott* is with us too."

"You're right, Zach. You are," she uttered softly. "The Lord always is."

She lingered in his arms momentarily before exiting the SUV. Walking into the ophthalmologist's office, Zach was thankful for Dr. Rubin's recommendation. Dr. Cooper's facility was immaculate and looked freshly painted. The office's pale blue, soft white and cream colors were as invitingly soothing as they could be.

The woman at the front desk who introduced herself as Cara was warm and friendly, and Leah seemed to relax some as she provided her personal information. Then, after a short wait, a technician called the woman of his heart back to the examination room. Walking tall with an air of courage and determined faith, Leah disappeared down the hallway.

Then it was his turn to wait and feel like everything was taking forever.

Each time the technician appeared in the waiting room and called out a visitor's name, he kept wishing it might be his. Finally, thinking Leah may not want him included in her results, he gave up on the idea.

Elbows on his knees and chin in his hands, he sat praying.

"Mr. Graber?"

His head popped up at the sound of his name. He could feel his heart pounding as he followed the now familiar-looking technician back to an office where the doctor and Leah were awaiting him. Even before sitting down in the chair offered to him, he glanced over at Leah. Unable to read her expression, his heart pounded even harder.

"Mr. Graber," Dr. Cooper greeted him. "It's nice to meet you."

"Happy to meet you too," he murmured.

"I've already gone over everything with Leah. But I asked Leah if there was anyone that she wanted me to share the results of her tests with as well. She said that would be you."

"I'm glad." He glanced at Leah and smiled. "And I'm ready to hear some *gut* news, Dr. Cooper."

"Well…" The doctor crossed her hands on the desktop and gave a wan smile. "How about if I start with the not-as-pleasant news first?"

Swallowing hard, he nodded.

"After our initial evaluation today, it would appear that Leah has a pituitary adenoma," she said matter-of-factly.

He blinked at the foreign word. "An *ada* what?"

"Adenoma. A pituitary tumor."

Zach did everything he could not to visibly flinch. "And so, what can you do? What does that mean?"

"It means that I'd like to refer Leah to a neuro-ophthalmologist who can work up her case with further tests, including an MRI. And then that specialist can refer to a neurosurgeon."

"A surgeon?" His heart literally skipped a beat. "Leah will need surgery?"

"The results from those additional tests will determine that, of course," Dr. Cooper replied. "But, if this is what I suspect, in all likelihood the tumor will be treated through surgery."

He paused for a moment, trying to take it all in. "And you said there's good news?"

"Yes, I did." The doctor nodded. "The good news is that this type of tumor is most always benign. And once removed and not pressing on the optic nerve as it is in Leah's case, some patients' vision returns fairly promptly, in days or weeks. That's not to say everyone's vision returns at absolutely one hundred percent. Still, overall, that's a positive outcome, don't you think?" The blond-haired physician smiled.

"Jah." He returned a grin before looking over at Leah. *"Jah,* it is."

"So before you two leave today, we'll provide you with information on the specialist in Cleveland that we feel would be best suited for this type of issue." She looked at Leah. "Which I believe is only about an hour and a half from your home in Sugarcreek."

"That's fine," Leah spoke up.

"Wherever you think is best is where we're going," Zach added.

"I do appreciate your confidence in me and our staff." Dr. Cooper gave a gracious smile.

"And tell Dr. Rubin I said hello the next time you see him, will you?"

"We will for sure," Leah replied.

At that point, Zach was grateful to notice a lighter lilt in Leah's voice. She sounded more hopeful than she had earlier. Even more, as they walked out of the office side by side, he was heartened when he looked at her. A rosy color was returning to her cheeks.

All along the return drive back to the farm, Leah could tell Zach was doing everything he could to make her feel comfortable and to keep things on her terms. He was listening when she needed to talk. He was talking when she needed him to share. He was positive when she began to have doubts. He even described lovely landscapes flashing outside the car window when he somehow knew she needed a reprieve from dwelling on herself.

By the time the car dropped them off in front of the Graber house —Ivan she knew was anxious to hear the results—Leah's heart was overflowing with thanks.

"Zach, before we go in… There's something I want to say."

"Okay." He leaned her way, poised to listen.

"Can we?" Without waiting for his answer, she tugged on his hand and as stably as she could manage, she led him to the side of Ivan's house. Coincidentally, they stood facing each other next to the fully bloomed hydrangea she'd hidden beside days before. The same place where she'd talked herself into letting him go from her life. The spot where she'd forbidden herself to be involved with him.

But now—her heart was without restraint.

"What is it?" he asked. "You're not thinking of not telling *Daed*, are you?"

"Oh, *nee*. Not at all. It's just…" She paused. "Well, I—I want to say…" she stammered.

He quirked a brow. *"Jah?"*

"Danke."

"You pulled me all the way over here to say that?" He chuckled. "And you don't have to say thank you, Leah. I hope you know by now that I'd do any—"

She lightly placed a finger on his lips, interrupting him. "I do know. But I still wanted to say it and to do this." Standing on her tiptoes, she gave him a quick peck on his cheek.

"Hmm." He frowned, tapping the spot her lips had barely touched. "That was so fast, I'm not sure I felt it."

She rolled her eyes. "You're picky, you know it?"

"Uh-huh, my pretty Leah. That's why I picked you."

Before she could exclaim over his compliment, he swung her into the circle of his arms, holding her snugly. Beyond a doubt, it was absolutely the place she'd longed to be.

"Oh, Zach." She uttered his name breathlessly, wrapping her arms around his neck. "Everything the doctor said today sounded encouraging. But if I do need surgery and it doesn't work out the way we hope, I don't want you to feel trapped because you feel sorry for me."

Removing a hand from around her waist, he gently caressed her cheek.

"Leah." He spoke her name softly, his gaze intent and sweet. "When are you ever going to understand? If I don't have you in my life, the only person I'll be feeling sorry for is me."

Disarmed, she couldn't help but trust the promise of his words. His captivating eyes only added to that feeling.

"Now…" He smiled at her. "All that being said, do you want to try whatever that fleeting sort of thing with your lips was again? And maybe you want to try to do it here?" He touched his mouth with his forefinger this time, causing her to laugh.

"Well, you're the expert at fixing things. Maybe you'd like to show me the right way first? But you'd better watch out. You know I'm a quick study," she added teasingly.

"Something tells me that's not a bad thing."

As he gathered her into his embrace again, she could feel her cheeks were all aglow. With the warmth of his closeness, how couldn't they be? And when his lips touched hers, the feel of his kiss was almost unbearable in its tenderness. Awakening a joyful heart within her, it was everything she'd imagined it would be. Surely, it was a kiss worth waiting for.

Chapter Seventeen

Zach sat in the Cleveland hospital waiting room, wringing his hands. Not only because of Leah's impending operation, which was worrisome enough. But in the deepest, most honest part of him, he was concerned about what he needed to tell her prior to the surgery. Which was taking a toll on him for sure.

The secret of who he really was and what he did for a living needed to be shared before he could ever propose to the woman of his dreams. All along he'd intended to ask for her hand in marriage before she underwent surgery. Because no matter the outcome of the operation, whether her vision was totally restored or not, he wanted to make certain of their life—their future—together.

Dismayed with himself, he shook his head. Why had he waited so long?

True, the weeks prior to the scheduled surgery had been busy. They'd traveled back and forth to Cleveland to see the neurological specialists there and then again for a pre-surgery examination. He'd contacted Highland Property Development to call off the deal. He'd also set up an appointment with Frieda Stoltz, who was excited about his father renting a space in her shop to be called "Horses' Haven." Maybe too excited, but his *daed* didn't seem to mind the pies that the single woman kept delivering to his house.

In the past days, there also hadn't been much of an opportunity to arrange quality time with Leah. Once Catherine spread the news about Leah's surgery, asking for prayers from everyone she knew, Leah had been tied up as well. Moms of her students, the students themselves and friends from worship streamed to her house daily, stopping by to wish her their best.

The other afternoon, however, when Leah asked him to escort her to their spot at the creek, he immediately thought it would a *wunderbaar* place to propose to her. Yet, as the warm water trickled around their soaking feet and the sun shone on their already warm clasped hands, instead of telling her who he really was, he froze.

He'd glanced at her sweet face and grew fearful of how she might respond to his truth. He told himself he needed the absolute best way to present what he wanted to say.

But now, glancing around the waiting room, he rubbed his forehead, still bewildered about what those right words might be.

Leah, do you want to know a secret about me?

No good. Why lead her in that direction?

Leah, what would you say if I told you...

Also not wise, when he couldn't predict her reaction.

Leah, you're the most beautiful woman in the world and you deserve...

All true. But flattery over honesty? That wasn't the right approach either.

Taking a deep breath, he realized what had to be done. He simply needed to be forthright. Steeling his shoulders, he braced himself, set on that decision. Until a nurse called his name, and the stuffing went right out of him.

"Zach? Would you like to come see Leah for a few minutes before we take her to surgery?"

The nurse led him to Leah's hospital room, and he readily stepped inside. Lying there in bed, his true love's eyes may have not been able to take in everything around her, but their hazel green hue still captivated him. The glow of her reddish-brown hair couldn't be hidden even when covered with a netted, puffy cap. And her full lips formed the smile that he knew so well. It tugged at his heart like always.

"You look beautiful," he whispered.

She giggled slightly. "Now who is going blind?"

"Leah…" He took her free hand, unwilling to hesitate any longer. "There's something I need to share with you. Something I know that I should've said long before this day."

"Oh, no, Zach. Please don't tell me you've been keeping something from me again. Not when I'm getting ready to go into surgery."

"Well…" He grimaced. "It's nothing too awful. Not bad at all really. The simple fact is, I've been wanting to tell you that I'm a rich man."

Even though she was already hooked up to an IV and couldn't easily get away from him, he felt pressed to grasp her hand more tightly.

"Aww." Her expression turned endearing. "That's so sweet of you to say."

He instantly realized she'd misinterpreted his confession and was about to leave it at that. But if his prayers came true and she'd agree to spend the rest of her life with him, that absolutely wouldn't work. Because if he also expected her to be able to trust him for the rest of their lives, there couldn't be secrets between them from the start.

"*Jah*, I am richer for having you in my life. That's so. You're the most precious gift *Gott* has ever given me." He kissed the back of her hand. "But, Leah, I'm—" He hesitated. "I'm also a rich man. A *wealthy* man."

"You mean money rich?" She blinked as shock registered on her face.

"*Jah*."

"How rich?"

"I'd say like..." He hedged. "Nearly a millionaire." He winced. Then promptly explained. "And I know you said that from your past experience, you don't like the idea of a man's focus being money. But the wealth *Gott* has gifted me with in my investments in Amish businesses, I promise you I use to help others."

There. He'd said it.

"And what's more," he continued, "I promise you, too, that if you'll say you'll marry me, Leah, that I will love you and cherish you for the rest of my life. And I'll never keep another secret from you, not ever."

There. He'd said that also. Gazing into her eyes, he waited for an answer.

And waited patiently some more, realizing it was truly a lot to process.

"Oh, Zach." She slipped her hand from his. Reaching up, she stroked his cheek. "I love you so…so much…" Her voice drifted.

"Is that a yes then?" He clasped his hand over hers, taking hold of it.

Suddenly, a nurse in royal blue scrubs swept into the room. "I'm sorry to interrupt you two, but it's time to head to surgery," she said, all businesslike.

"And my name is…" Leah murmured. "Lee…ahh. Zooo…k."

"I know, dear, I asked you your name and date of birth earlier, remember?" The nurse smiled before turning to him. "May I?" she asked, before removing Leah's hand from his so she could gently place it at Leah's side.

"And my birthday is…" Leah started up again. "It's… Hmm…" Her eyelids began to close.

"It's November twenty-fifth," Zach said, also supplying the year.

"Ohhh…" Leah's eyes fluttered open slightly. "He remembers my birthday," she crooned. "He's so cute…isn't he? So cute I could bottle him up in a mason jar."

Zach could feel his face redden while the nurse simply grinned. "She's getting drowsy from the IV. We gave her something to relax her," the nurse informed him. "No need to be embarrassed. That was very sweet compared to some things I hear." She laughed.

With that, the nurse hoisted up the bedside bars and unlocked the brakes on the bed. Before she began pushing the bed out the door, she turned to him.

"As soon as Leah is in recovery, we'll call you back so the surgeon can speak with you. Then when she's stable and awake, you can be with her again."

"All right. Thank you."

Following behind the rolling bed transporting the woman he loved, he wished again and again he could've, would've, told her more. And sooner. So much sooner.

Epilogue

~

One year later

Leah stilled the rocking chair she was sitting in and the nursery grew silent. She gazed adoringly at the precious, sleeping baby boy nestled in her arms. Overwhelmed with emotion, a tingling sensation floated over her cheeks and grateful tears misted her eyes. And yet she could still see clearly. So clearly.

Praise You, Heavenly Father, praise You!

"Joshua," she whispered, "I know I've told you what I see when I look at you. But you won't mind if I say my short verse again, will you, sweet boy?" She smiled down at him. "I see ten tiny toes to tickle. A button nose I love to dot with a kiss. And do you know when your blue eyes—like your *daed*'s—smile into mine, they fill my world with bliss?" She paused and sighed wistfully. "Oh, darling *buwe*, I could sit and stare at you all night."

Her infant's rosy cheek twitched as if in response to her endearment, causing her to smile again. "You have me wrapped around your tiny finger already, don't you?"

"I know that feeling well, my lovely *frau*," Zach said quietly as he sauntered into his refurbished former bedroom and kissed the top of her *kapp*. "How's our little one doing?"

"Oh, he's fine and fast asleep. It's me who has the problem," she whispered. "I can't make myself put him down."

In the glow of the lamp, she could see Zach bite back a grin. "*Jah*, our boy has you wrapped around his finger. Me too. But he's worth it, ain't so?" He beamed.

"I suppose we should put him in his crib, shouldn't we?" She lifted herself up from the rocker.

"Here." Her husband outstretched his arms. "I'll take him."

She watched as Zach gently settled Joshua into his crib. Then it should have been time for them to slip out from the room. Even so, as a stream of moonlight poured in the window, they were transfixed. They stood over the crib, staring at their cherished blessing some more.

"Oh, Zach, every minute of the day I'm so

thankful to the Lord for our son." Droplets filled her eyes again. "And so thankful that I can see him."

"I know." He wrapped his arm around her shoulder, drawing her close. "But even if you couldn't have, you still would've felt our Joshua. You would've embraced him and loved him. A mother's heart is like that. Your heart is like that."

His sweetness always touched her deeply. She placed a hand on his chest, snuggling into him even more. "You know, I can't wait until my sister's family comes for the Swiss Festival in a few weeks and they get to meet him. And that's about the same time Cat and Thomas's baby will be arriving too."

"It'll be good for Joshua to have a cousin right next door to grow up with."

"*Jah*, I'm so glad they decided to make their home there. And when they're older, the two *kinner* can play in the creek, right close to Ivan's new house."

"Don't forget, Joshua will have Matthew and Anna's family to love him too. Not to mention your students and their moms who keep mailing books to him." He smiled.

"He's one blessed boy, isn't he?"

"I'm thinking it runs in the family," Zach said matter-of-factly.

After a final moment of gazing at their son, Leah turned off the lamp and Zach took her hand as they walked from the room. They'd barely gotten halfway down the hall when they heard someone at the front door.

"Wonder who that is?" Zach asked.

"It's your *daed* and Frieda."

"You knew they were coming?"

"*Jah.* They're bringing something special."

"How come you know about it and I don't?"

She pursed her lips to hold back a smile. "I guess because it's a secret."

"But I thought we agreed to no more secrets."

"We did. But then there you went secretly opening The Book Nook for me in town," she reminded him.

"That wasn't a secret. It was a late wedding gift."

"Well, this is a gift too. Mostly for Joshua, but I'm sure you'll appreciate it."

When she'd peeked in on Ivan while he was working on the rocking horse he was carving for Joshua, she'd seen it come to life in various stages. There was no denying he'd carved the toy to look like the horse that Zach had named Bear.

"Now you have me curious," Zach said. "You're still not going to tell me?"

"I'll let you in on one thing…" She crooked her finger for him to come close, and watched his eyes grow wide with expectation. "It's no secret that I love you."

He chuckled as he grabbed her hand, whirling her around until she was curled into his broad chest. Lifting her chin to meet his gaze, he spoke softly, "That goes for me too. There isn't a day that goes by, my beautiful *frau*, that I don't wake up in the morning or go to sleep at night without thanking *Gott* for bringing you into my life."

"Oh, Zach." She sighed. "I thank *Gott* too."

He inclined his head to kiss her. But before his lips touched hers, she knew in her heart that every word he'd said was true. She could hear it in the sweet tone of his voice. But most of all, she could see the undeniable love he had for her in his eyes.

* * * * *

Dear Reader,

I was so happy while penning Leah and Zach's story because it took me back to Sugarcreek, and not just in spirit or through sweet memories. As it happened, my critique partners (and dear friends) decided Ohio Amish country would be the perfect spot for a writing retreat. How could I disagree?

In the four days we spent in a rustic cabin we got ideas fleshed out and chapters written too. But we also laughed, shared, celebrated and ate more snacks than we should have.

I'm telling you this because coming home I thought how the chance to know and share with these special women might have never happened. Many years ago, I almost didn't say yes to their invitation to join their critique group. I'd been working in a creative field but writing a book was something new, and they were so far ahead of me. Can I tell you that as I sit typing this and tears mist my eyes I'm so thankful I shared my writing and myself with them?

As just noted, like Leah and Zach, I know it's not always easy to open up and to trust. But, also like the two of them, I've learned when I do trust God and the special people He sends into my life, those relationships can be beyond rewarding.

I hope all is well in your corner of the world! If you'd like to say hello sometime, visit me at my website www.cathyliggett.com or on Facebook.

Blessings to you now and always,
Cathy

Get 4 FREE REWARDS!

We'll send you 2 FREE Books plus 2 FREE Mystery Gifts.

FREE Value Over **$20**

Both the **Love Inspired®** and **Love Inspired® Suspense** series feature compelling novels filled with inspirational romance, faith, forgiveness, and hope.

YES! Please send me 2 FREE novels from the Love Inspired or Love Inspired Suspense series and my 2 FREE gifts (gifts are worth about $10 retail). After receiving them, if I don't wish to receive any more books, I can return the shipping statement marked "cancel." If I don't cancel, I will receive 6 brand-new Love Inspired Larger-Print books or Love Inspired Suspense Larger-Print books every month and be billed just $6.24 each in the U.S. or $6.49 each in Canada. That is a savings of at least 17% off the cover price. It's quite a bargain! Shipping and handling is just 50¢ per book in the U.S. and $1.25 per book in Canada.* I understand that accepting the 2 free books and gifts places me under no obligation to buy anything. I can always return a shipment and cancel at any time by calling the number below. The free books and gifts are mine to keep no matter what I decide.

Choose one: ☐ **Love Inspired** Larger-Print (122/322 IDN GRDF)   ☐ **Love Inspired Suspense** Larger-Print (107/307 IDN GRDF)

Name (please print)

Address   Apt. #

City   State/Province   Zip/Postal Code

Email: Please check this box ☐ if you would like to receive newsletters and promotional emails from Harlequin Enterprises ULC and its affiliates. You can unsubscribe anytime.

Mail to the **Harlequin Reader Service:**
IN U.S.A.: P.O. Box 1341, Buffalo, NY 14240-8531
IN CANADA: P.O. Box 603, Fort Erie, Ontario L2A 5X3

Want to try 2 free books from another series? Call 1-800-873-8635 or visit www.ReaderService.com.

---

*Terms and prices subject to change without notice. Prices do not include sales taxes, which will be charged (if applicable) based on your state or country of residence. Canadian residents will be charged applicable taxes. Offer not valid in Quebec. This offer is limited to one order per household. Books received may not be as shown. Not valid for current subscribers to the Love Inspired or Love Inspired Suspense series. All orders subject to approval. Credit or debit balances in a customer's account(s) may be offset by any other outstanding balance owed by or to the customer. Please allow 4 to 6 weeks for delivery. Offer available while quantities last.

Your Privacy—Your information is being collected by Harlequin Enterprises ULC, operating as Harlequin Reader Service. For a complete summary of the information we collect, how we use this information and to whom it is disclosed, please visit our privacy notice located at corporate.harlequin.com/privacy-notice. From time to time we may also exchange your personal information with reputable third parties. If you wish to opt out of this sharing of your personal information, please visit readerservice.com/consumerschoice or call 1-800-873-8635. **Notice to California Residents**—Under California law, you have specific rights to control and access your data. For more information on these rights and how to exercise them, visit corporate.harlequin.com/california-privacy.

LIRLIS22R2

COUNTRY LEGACY COLLECTION

19 FREE BOOKS IN ALL!

Cowboys, adventure and romance await you in this new collection! Enjoy superb reading all year long with books by bestselling authors like Diana Palmer, Sasha Summers and Marie Ferrarella!

YES! Please send me the **Country Legacy Collection!** This collection begins with 3 FREE books and 2 FREE gifts in the first shipment. Along with my 3 free books, I'll also get 3 more books from the **Country Legacy Collection**, which I may either return and owe nothing or keep for the low price of $24.60 U.S./$28.12 CDN each plus $2.99 U.S./$7.49 CDN for shipping and handling per shipment*. If I decide to continue, about once a month for 8 months, I will get 6 or 7 more books but will only pay for 4. That means 2 or 3 books in every shipment will be FREE! If I decide to keep the entire collection, I'll have paid for only 32 books because 19 are FREE! I understand that accepting the 3 free books and gifts places me under no obligation to buy anything. I can always return a shipment and cancel at any time. My free books and gifts are mine to keep no matter what I decide.

☐ 275 HCK 1939   ☐ 475 HCK 1939

Name (please print)

Address   Apt. #

City   State/Province   Zip/Postal Code

Mail to the Harlequin Reader Service:
IN U.S.A.: P.O. Box 1341, Buffalo, NY 14240-8571
IN CANADA: P.O. Box 603, Fort Erie, Ontario L2A 5X3

50BOOKCL22

HARLEQUIN
PLUS

Announcing a **BRAND-NEW** multimedia subscription service for romance fans like you!

Read, Watch and Play.

Experience the easiest way to get the romance content you crave.

Start your **FREE 7 DAY TRIAL** at
<u>www.harlequinplus.com/freetrial</u>.